PRAISE FOR *DOGMA*

"Uproarious." —*NEW YORK TIMES BOOK REVIEW*

"[*Dogma*] brings back W. and Lars, the most unlikely and absurd literary duo since Samuel Beckett's Vladimir and Estragon. . . . Like Godot, this novel is a philosophical rumination, at once serious and playful, on the nature of existence and meaning. While it's comic, there is at bottom a profoundly tragic sense of the chaos and emptiness of modern life. Despair has rarely been so entertaining." —*LIBRARY JOURNAL*

"Just when my hilarity over the first book of their misadventures, *Spurious*, had faded to a low chuckle, *Dogma* comes along. Between the two books, there's almost no point in breathing, much less coming to any strong conclusions about life, the universe, and everything."
—*LOS ANGELES REVIEW OF BOOKS*

"Witheringly, gut-bustingly funny." —*THE NEW INQUIRY*

"*Dogma*, like its prequel *Spurious*, is provocative in its arguments, scrupulously plain in its style and excoriating in its honesty. Iyer is an author who rejects the parochialism and timidity we too often associate with British novelists in favour of an ugly grapple with the big themes."
—*THE SPECTATOR* (UK)

"The epithet 'Beckettian' is perhaps the most overused in criticism, frequently employed as a proxy for less distinguished designations such as 'sparse' or 'a bit depressing'. But Lars Iyer's fiction richly deserves this appellation. His playfully spare—and wryly depressing—landscape, incorporating a bickering double act on a hopeless, existential journey, is steeped in the bathos, farce, wordplay and metaphysics of the man John Calder referred to as 'the last of the great stoics', its characters accelerating towards a condition of eternal silence, fuelled only by the necessity of speaking out." —*THE TIMES LITERARY SUPPLEMENT*

"The bathos is perfectly pitched, and Lars and W.'s antics are gloriously uproarious." —DAVID WINTERS, *THE RUMPUS*

"Expertly crafted throughout… *Dogma* is also constantly in the process of becoming, which is why—for all the talk of exhaustion and Armageddon—it feels so vital and remarkably angst-free…. a comic celebration." —ANDREW GALLIX, *BOOKSLUT*

"Iyer has distinguished himself as a writer of great comic ability, and I would certainly snap up anything else he might write to see how he deploys this blend of erudition and wit." —JACOB SILVERMAN, *THE QUARTERLY CONVERSATION*

"Happily, the insults are Falstafian (as in *Spurious*)… *Dogma*'s aphoristic style makes the urge to frequently quote from it irresistible." —*THE INDIAN EXPRESS*

"Iyer employs the first-person perspective with fantastic flair and originality…. this book is surreal, brainy, plotless, and arguably pointless. It is also brilliantly written and very funny…. I don't know who else might like this strange book as much as I did, but, as for me, I can't wait for the third." —DREW NELLINS, *THE MILLIONS*

"Like its predecessor, *Dogma* is above all a goldmine of ingeniously abstruse insults, and as a result it is frequently piss-yourself-on-public-transport hilarious." —DANNY BYRNE, *READY, STEADY, BOOK*

PRAISE FOR *SPURIOUS*

EXODUS

EXODUS

....

Lars Iyer

MELVILLE HOUSE
BROOKLYN · LONDON

EXODUS

First Melville House Printing: December 2012

Cover photograph by William Hundley

Melville House Publishing
145 Plymouth Street
Brooklyn, New York 11201

mhpbooks.com

ISBN: 978-1-61219-182-9

Manufactured in the United States of America
1 2 3 4 5 6 7 8 9 10

Library of Congress Cataloging-in-Publication Data

Iyer, Lars.
  Exodus / Lars Iyer.
      pages cm
  ISBN 978-1-61219-182-9
  1. Philosophy--Fiction. 2. Black humor (Literature) I. Title.
  PR6109.Y47E96 2013
  823'.92--dc23
                                            2012041220

He has things to tell me, W. says when I meet him at Newcastle airport in the morning. Great things! But first he needs a pint. He needs to regroup.

W.'s plane was full of obese children, he says. — 'When did everyone get so fat?' They ran up and down the aisle, unhindered by their girth. But W. got down to some reading despite their bellowing. He underlined passages and wrote in his notebook.

And what was I reading, as I waited for him? When I tell him, he nods and murmurs. — 'Mazzarri, oh I see. Flusser, ah that's far too complex for Lars...'

I'll have to pay for the beer, W. says in *The Trent*. He no longer carries money, he says. He's like the Queen.

W. wonders why I always make my lips — my great fat lips — into a funnel as I lift my drink. No doubt it's all the better to pour it down, pint after pint: a funnel for the two pints I always neck at the bar before I sit down, and for the dregs of pints that other people leave behind...

A legal technicality, W. says over his second pint. Sacked by his university when they closed down the humanities, and what saved him? *A legal technicality.*

It's not as if he hadn't tried to defend himself, W. says. On the contrary, he'd mounted a heroic defence! At his termination hearing he performed a great oration, his version of Socrates's apology to the jurists of Athens. How he spoke!, W. says. Hours and hours without cease! The committee groaned, they slept. They tried to interrupt, begged to adjourn, but each time W. simply held up his hand. *He wasn't done*.

He showed charts and circulated handouts, W. says. He pushed his *Summa Idiotica* across the table: four hundred pages to make the case against his dismissal. Chapters! An index! A table of contents! Twenty-four appendices! It will stand as his finest work, W. says. But it was all for nothing.

A *legal technicality*, W. says. That's what saved him. Which is ironic, because it was through a *legal technicality* that they tried to get rid of him.

His Union uncovered it. Something about the way the college management had had him marched off campus, when they suspected him of sedition... Something about interfering with his freedom of movement, with his freedom of *speech*... W. had a case for *legal action* against the College, his Union said. He could create *bad PR* for the College. Bad press!... At a stroke, W. was unsackable.

A *legal technicality*. It's the *contingency* of his salvation that bothers him, W. says. He was saved, but he might not have been. And if he was saved, it wasn't because of anything he'd done. It wasn't because of *fate*, or *grace*. It wasn't because of his apology. It wasn't because he'd been *chosen* in some way...

But he's going to act as though he *was* chosen, W. says. As though he *was* saved by grace. As though a divine mission has been allotted to him.

That's what our lecture tour is to be about, W.'s decided. Our great lecture tour of Great Britain, our last look at the ruins of the humanities. We are to investigate the *conditions of his sacking*!, W. says. The conditions of the destruction of philosophy at his university — of the destruction of philosophy in Britain — of the destruction of philosophy in the whole world! The end days are upon us, and we must witness them at first hand, W. says. The Pharoah is drowning the children of philosophy. — 'Drink up, fat boy!, there's not much time'.

Newcastle. My office. The collected works of Kierkegaard, spanning the windowsill. W.'s always admired them — their sober spines, the different colours against which their titles appear, varying from volume to volume (*Point of View* in charcoal, *The Book on Adler* in bronze, *Fear and Trembling* in a handsome burgundy). And then there's the sheer bulk of them, with my improvised bookmarks sticking out at random. — 'You mean you've actually read something!' W says.

And I have read them. The books look worn, tired. — 'Is that blood?', W. wonders, of the blotches in the margins of *Practice in Christianity*. 'Are those tears?' There are even annotations, W. notices. 'What did you write?', W. asks, turning the book sideways. He can hardly make out a line. *Iration* — what does that mean? *Livity* — what is that?

Why is it that Kierkegaard attracts lunatics?, W. says. He's seen it before, with some of his more desperate students. The half-wild ones, who've come off the streets after years of destitution. The half-mad ones, who want only to lose themselves in some great task of scholarship, but who are made for anything but a great task of scholarship...

In truth, I know more about Kierkegaard than he does, W. admits. It's my Danish connection. Of course, I'm only *half* Danish, W. says. Half Danish and half Indian, a peculiar combination, he says. He, of course, is Irish on one side of his family and from Jewish stock — *Ostjude* stock — on the other. The wrong background for Kierkegaard, W. says.

But he wants to understand Kierkegaard, W. says. Kierkegaard's become fateful to him. Kierkegaard is the *philosopher of despair*, W. says, and it's *despair* we'll have to think, if we're to confront the closure of philosophy departments in Britain. It's the *philosopher of despair* we'll have to read, if we're to grasp the conditions of that closure, which is to say, *capitalism itself*.

I'm to be his guide in the mountains of Kierkegaard, W. says. His sherpa. I'm to carry his things. What should he bring? His *learning*, W. says. His years of study in the philosophy of religion. He'll instruct me as we climb, W. says. He'll point things out, and when he gets tired, I can give him a piggy-back.

'God, what a racket! How do you do any work?', W. says.

The sound of drilling, high pitched, then lower pitched as they cut through something. The fizz of a lorry's brakes. The clattering of metal poles being thrown onto metal poles. A heavy chugging in the distance. The faraway throbbing of engines...

They're rebuilding the campus, I tell W. They're putting up new office blocks for the private partners of the university.

He requires silence when he works, W. says. Silence and calm, in his study in the pre-dawn morning, just the pigeons flapping their wings and cooing to annoy him, and Sal asleep in the other room.

Stand well clear, vehicle reversing: a warning from a tannoyed male voice. And now warnings overlapping with warnings, as many vehicles reverse: *Stand well clear... Stand well clear... Stand well clear...* And now a high pitched throb, very loud, like a helicopter landing. — 'Surely a helicopter isn't landing?', W. says. 'A helicopter couldn't be landing...'

We walk out through the campus, through the narrow pedestrian routes left to us alongside the building works. W. feels so *channelled*, he says. We're being *route-marched*, he says, staff and student alike, heads down and in lock-step. — 'Where are they leading us?', he says. 'Where are we going?'

A thick smell — is it tar? They must be pouring tar. They must be making some kind of route for the lorries. A hiss, as of gas escaping. The high beeping of a reversing vehicle. — 'They're going to crush us!', W. says.

We emerge safely into the quadrangle. — 'They're going to crush us', W. repeats calmly. What use is philosophy to the private partners of the university? What use will it be to the new breed of the university, which is busy hatching from the old one?

'How long do you think we'll last?', W. says. 'How long before philosophy is destroyed altogether?' Because there's no room for us in this world, he says. No room for Kierkegaard and for scholars of Kierkegaard...

'Are they shredding trees?', W. asks, as we look back at the building works. Yes, they really are: we can see them cutting off the boughs with chainsaws, and feeding them into huge machines. Leaves fly up over the fence. And the smell: sap. The stuff of life, W. says, being shredded.

It'll be our turn next, W. says. They'll cut off our arms and legs and feed us into the huge machines...

Stand well clear... Stand well clear...

The Town Moor: escape. We wander through the knee-high grass. What are those birds?, we wonder. What are those flowers? But we have no idea.

The Moor is like the world on the fifth day of creation, we agree — before Adam, before anyone, when everything went unnamed and unredeemed. It needs words, we agree. It needs a poet! Where is the *Rilke of Newcastle* to sing of the Moor?

Above us, a shore of clouds and then blue sky. — 'That's a weather front', W. says. Which way is it travelling? Where is it heading? And where are *we* heading, we who walk beneath the shore of clouds?

Is the future open to us, or closed? W. can never decide. Are we making progress, or falling behind? W. can never decide that, either.

Alcoholics in the long grass, stretching their limbs and laughing, half-drunk bottles of cider by their ankles. Anyone can walk on the Town Moor, he likes that, W. says. Where the alcoholic can walk, *he* walks, W. says. And where the alcoholic cannot walk — where his way is barred by security guards or policemen — W. will not walk either.

Should we lie down in the long grass and drink ourselves to death?, we wonder. Should we just give up — give up everything — and let death come and find us on the Town Moor? But we consider ourselves to have *work to do* — that's our idiocy, and our salvation. We actually take ourselves to be *busy* — that's our imposture and our chance of survival.

W. remembers how it all began. I came into his care, like a Robin to his Batman: a ward, a protégé. How was he to know what would happen?

He taught me table manners as best he could. He tried to teach me politeness — to shake hands, to make chit-chat. He stopped me from continually touching my skin through my shirt, and tried to quieten my bellowing.

Friendship involves a lot of nagging, W. says. I had to be nagged! I was like a prisoner, released blinking into the light. What had I known of life, before I met him? How had I survived?

I was a scholarly *Kasper Hauser*, W. says, who knew nothing of reading, or note-taking. I could read, that much is true. But only just, only approximately, and with a great deal of pathos, with wild underlinings and illegitimate identifications. — 'You thought every book you read was about you, didn't you?' That's me!, I would say, pointing to a passage in Hegel. It's about me!, I would say, pointing to the *Science of Logic*.

And all along, W. was waiting to see if I was the harbourer of some secret wisdom, if my *years of unemployment* had taught me some great and unguessable insight. He took me out into the scholarly world. People were impressed at first, then frightened. Why is he covered in his own spittle?, they asked. Why is he covering us with his spittle?

I made audiences flinch, W. says. Professors would turn white, or leave to vomit. — 'They couldn't understand what had just happened'. But W. understood. His heart leaped up.

Hadn't he always sought an *outsider scholar*? Hadn't he always dreamt of intellectual movements that took place *outside the university*? Of professors of desperation; of the university of alcoholism?

I came from the outside, and I brought the outside with me, W. says. I came from the everyday and had to stamp the everyday from my boots. — 'How long had you been unemployed?' Years, I tell him. Years!: W. can't imagine it. — 'And for how long before that had you worked in your warehouse?' Years again. — 'Years!', W. exclaims. Of course, there was also my time with the monks. Ah yes, my ever-surprising *monk years*, W. says.

But there you were, and who had seen anything like it? — 'You were like a one man horde, a Tartar'. There was spittle on my lips and drool in my beard. Had I ever heard of a footnote? Did I know what an appendix was, or what *op. cit.* might mean? Scholarly standards were an irrelevance to me; academic conventions an imposition I could completely ignore. It was quite impressive.

'Your book! Your first book!' W.'s still amazed. It was entirely without scholarship, without ideas, W. says. Without the usual concern to explain or to clarify. A book almost entirely lacking in merit. And yet! W. saw something there, although no one else did. He saw it, and not in spite of its many typos and printing errors... It was there *because* of them, W. says. It was inextricable from them: a kind of massive, looming incompetence. A cloud of stupidity covering the sun, and belonging to it like its shadow.

It was demonic, W. says. It was as forceful as a demiurge. That's when he became aware of it as a kind of *un*God, as a division of darkness within light, of death within life. How could anything so bad have been written? Who could have defiled the temple of scholarship and revealed it to have been always defiled? He saw it, W. says, even if no one else did. And it was his role to look after me, until the very end.

Spital Tongues, Newcastle. There it is, W. says, as we walk past the allotments. There it is, the terrace where my flat is buried. The dampest row of flats there ever was, W. says. The dampest Tyneside flats, built atop a culvetted river, atop a coal tunnel now used for sewage, atop old mine workings, now full of water. The dampest, most rat-infested flats, which should have been demolished a hundred years ago, but have been allowed to survive in their degradation. The last of the slums after all the slums have been cleared...

And there's *my* flat, the centre of the catastrophe, W. says. *My* flat, a swamp in the shape of a flat, a flat-plague, interred in its pit. *My* flat that the sun doesn't reach, deep underground like a mausoleum to the world's greatest idiot. *My* flat, like a barrow for the greatest of imbeciles...

'What possessed you to buy an underground flat?' W. says. To be close to the earth, he says, was that it? To be close to the toads and the worms, to the creatures of the earth?

Slug trails along the floorboards... Curled up woodlice in room corners... — 'The flat's being taken back by nature', W. says. He's right. The walls are green. Mushrooms grow from the ceiling. And then there's the damp, of course. The ever-present damp. Is it alive? Is it dead? It's beyond life, and beyond death, W. says.

They should send scientists out to study it, my damp, W. says. They should try to *communicate* with it, like the scientists in *Solaris*. It's more intelligent than us, W. says, he's sure of it. My damp has something momentous to say, something profound. In fact, isn't it speaking now, to those who have ears to hear? Isn't it rumbling in the darkness? I should know, W. says. I live with it. — 'You understand the damp', W. says. Or rather, the damp understands itself in me.

And there are the rats, too, he shouldn't forget them. *My* rats, that's how he thinks of them. My rats, my familiars, living under my floorboards. He'd hear them chattering if he pressed his ear to the floor, W. knows that. He'd hear them speaking their obscene language, for all that I tell him the rats are all dead.

What next?, W. wonders. What will be the next plague? There are the slugs, of course, but they're scarcely a plague. There are the ants — and the mushrooms. But he believes something more dreadful is gathering itself in my flat, W. says. Something Lovecraftian. Something *cosmic*…

He's never seen plants growing directly out of concrete, except in my yard, W. says. It's quite extraordinary. It's Japanese knotweed, I tell him. Oh yes, he heard something about it on the radio, W. says. Isn't it taking over Britain? Isn't it choking all our native species one by one? Well, now he knows where it's coming from, W. says. — 'Your yard is the source of all evil'.

My living room. W. takes his place on the Chair of Judgement: 'Bring me gin!' It's going to be a long night. He has a lot to get through, W. says, leaning his chair back against the wall.

My failings, my failures: the usual topic. The failure of my life, of my thought. The failure of my books. Familiar topics. My past failures, my present ones: yes we know about those, W. says. But my *future* failings ... that's what W. wants to talk about tonight.

'Where will you have gone wrong?', he says. 'What will you have done? What crimes have you yet to commit? How will you have managed to have failed anew?'

It's quite a tense, isn't it, the future perfect?, W. says. Who *will I have* disappointed? Him, of course, W. says. Whose hopes *will I have* defiled? His, of course, W. says. His hopes.

Ah, what will I have done to him, W., in the future? What terrors await him? — 'Will you have written another book? Will you have come up with another escape plan?' Ah, but he knows what will have happened. *I* know. We'll have been sacked, and living on the dole.

He only teaches sports science students, now they've closed the humanities at his college, W. says. They arrive at his seminars ruddy-faced and healthy looking, with towels around their necks. He does his best to improve them, W. says, but it's no good.

They're keen in their way, his students, W. says. They want to do well. But he's having trouble impressing them with the *majesty of thinking*. He's having trouble making them understand the *despair of the world*.

At least there are still a few of his postgraduates around, W. says. At least he still has some allies. One day, they might make a last stand, W. says. They might occupy the gym and trample the cricket pitch. He's been trying to encourage them.

And in the meantime? He roams the corridors that used to echo with the great names. He walks through the empty quadrangle where he used to talk Kant with his colleagues. He sits alone in the refectory, where fellow scholars used to discuss Luhmann and Ellul over their sandwiches, and wanders past the empty offices where he used to have reading groups with other academics, puzzling over Prigogine together, pondering Michel Serres...

Of course, they're going to close all humanities courses in British universities, W. says. It's like the '80s over again: protests and strikes, departmental closures and redundancies. It was a terrible time, W. says.

But at least the government recognised philosophy as the enemy in the '80s, W. says. At least they understood the power of philosophy. The humanities are the enemy of capitalism: that's what they understood in the '80s. Philosophy is the eternal adversary of capitalism...

But now? The government no longer understands the humanities as an enemy, W. says. The government has nothing in particular against philosophy. They do not oppose it on ideological grounds, nor because they suspect it of *subversion*. They are not concerned that philosophy is training *insurgents of thought*.

They're simply going to *marketise education*, W. says. They're simply going to turn the university over to the free market, just as they are turning all sectors of the public services over to the free market. They're going to submit philosophy to the *forces of capitalism*...

Sometimes, W. is tempted by the idea that philosophy might be *liberated* by its destruction. That, extinguished in the universities, philosophy might soar into its own sky, free of every institutional encumbrance.

Perhaps there will be a new age of thinker-Cynics, former academics, living on the streets and *speaking truth to power*, W. thinks. Perhaps new Socrateses will question empty-headed yuppies in the marketplace...

But then W. reminds himself that in the future, the streets will be sold off, and all public spaces privatised. That the empty-headed yuppie is only a *function of the system*. That capitalism has no face, and that the financial markets are only a *simmering chaos*.

What kind of Cynic could speak truth to a function? What new Socrates could be a gadfly to *simmering chaos*?

Reading his redundancy letter, W. felt like the dying Rutger Hauer in *Bladerunner*, he says. '*I've seen things you people wouldn't believe*', Hauer said to his murderers. '*Attack ships off the shoulder of Orion. C-beams glittering in the dark near Tannhauser Gate...*' Hasn't W. seen things his sackers wouldn't believe? He's leant on a piano at which Cornelius Castioriadis sang revolutionary songs, at an Essex postgraduate party. He's watched Jean-François Courtine in full flight, writing in Arabic on a Sorbonne blackboard, from right to left. He's heard the legend of Chouchani, from Levinas's own lips, over cups of tea in a Paris apartment...

Didn't his managers understand what he'd seen?, W. says. Didn't they know that he was part of the legendary generation of *Essex postgraduates*?

Morning. Leazes Park, Newcastle. This is where I should come when the ping of incoming emails depresses me, W. says. I should rest my gaze on the waterfowl: the black-headed geese, the kingly swans. I should hire a rowing boat to take a turn around the lake. Above all, I should walk...

A man must walk if he is to think, W. says. We have to be receptive to thoughts, open to them; an idea might come to us at any time, and it's only when we relax — when we let the mind stretch out — that it can reach us. How many times has W. walked out alone, hoping that an idea would come looking for him?

W. goes to the tulip garden at Mount Edgcumbe when he wants to think, he says. Off he sets in the morning, with his Kafka and a notebook in his man bag, heading up to the Naval dockyards, and then catching the ferry across the Tamar. On the other side, it is only a short walk to the tulip garden, which he approaches through the orangery, then the English garden and then the French garden, he says. But it is the tulip garden which is his destination, W. says, whether it's spring or summer, or, for that matter, autumn or winter; whether or not there is anything in flower.

We must not so much look for ideas, W. says, as let ideas find us. It is not a question of *mental effort*, but of *mental slacken-ing*, he says. Ideas need *time* to emerge — unmeasured time. Ideas despise clocks. They even despise notebooks.

Lately, W. has been deliberately neglecting his notebooks. He's put them aside, he says, all the better for ideas to reach him. W.'s even been neglecting himself! Is it any accident that Solomon Maimon was taken for a vagrant?

Is it because he thought I was a thinker-vagrant that he was drawn to me?, W. wonders. I was certainly scruffy enough, unkempt enough... But these signs of vagabondage were unaccompanied by signs of thought. The vagrant is not necessarily a thinker: it was a painful lesson, W. says.

Solomon Maimon was dirty!: that's what I always protest to W. when he reprimands me for my personal habits. But Maimon was a genius!, W. cries. A genius driven out of his home city for daring to philosophise. A beggar-genius living on alms, as he wandered for years before being offered a posi-tion as a tutor.

Was it in those years that Maimon formulated the most decisive criticisms of Kantian thought that have been made? Was it then, his begging bowl before him, and Kant's three critiques in his knapsack, that ideas came to him, which, in his final years, he would publish in a series of essays?

Only Maimon understands me, Kant said, after reading his unkempt admirer's *Transcendental Philosophy* in manu-script. And when Kant died, it was suspected that among the causes of his death was Maimon's devastating criticism of his work. How could he, Kant, survive an attack by the *ragged philosopher*?

But Maimon never succeeded in penetrating academic circles, nor even the salons of enlightened Berlin Jews. To them he was of the *Ostjude*, his manners too rough, his jerks and tics too disconcerting, his speech stammering and garbled. And he was a *difficult* man, lacking in manners, brusque and intolerant when he should have been diplomatic.

And he smelt awful, everyone said that. *Maimon stinks! Get him out of here!*: that's what you'd hear in Berlin salons. And out he went, back onto the frozen streets, back outside with the three critiques in his knapsack...

Maimon was an alcoholic, of course. He drank like a madman, W. says. He drank himself to death even when he found employment as a tutor, even as great essay after great essay poured forth from his pen.

Is that what's going to happen to me? Am I going to produce a great stream of books in *my* final years, which can't be far off?, W. says. He's offered me support, and now he's waiting. He brought me in from the cold, and now he's sitting by expectantly. But he thinks he's going to be disappointed.

W. stops to read the plaque about waterfowl. There's usually a melancholy to the urban park, he says, but Leazes Park is different. It's more vibrant, somehow. We look around us: the empty bandstand, the high wall of St James's Park, goths and emo kids drinking cider in the sun… It all harbours some great clue to life, W.'s strangely certain about that, or maybe it's the effect of the coffee I made for him this morning.

We should bring *our thinkers* here, W. says, the ones we hope will become our leaders of thought. This is the perfect place to help them walk away from their troubles. It's the perfect place to help them *walk their way to thought*.

Haven't we taken many walks alongside one or other of our thinkers? Haven't we been able to loosen our thinkers from the crowd and *take them outside*?

Thinkers have thanked us for nothing less: for giving them freedom from the crowd. Crowds are unbearable to the real thinker, W. says. The thinker always wants to escape. And so we've taken many such journeys — journeys out, away from the others, in company with one or other of our thinkers. Away from the tumult.

We try to calm our thinkers on such walks, that's our main task, W. notes. We try to put them at ease, drawing attention to the pleasant vistas around us, to the blueness of the sky, to the peace of the forest. We make no demands. It's not about us: we've always grasped that.

Occasionally, W. says, I've begun to expound my *caffeine theories*, and he has to put a stop to it. He prods me when our thinker isn't looking. He raises his finger to his lips. And occasionally, W. ventures to introduce some intellectual topic or other before pulling himself back, apologising.

Let the thinker introduce the topic!, we've always told ourselves. And sometimes they do. Sometimes they begin to speak, and we respond only to enable them to speak some more, only to let ourselves drift into the central current of their reflections.

What a privilege it is to hear a thinker think! To hear the latest ideas of a thinker extemporised to us as to no one in particular! To be the beach upon which the thinker-sea spreads its waves! To be the shore over which the thought-ocean breaks!

Of course, we can understand little of what we hear. But we expect nothing more. In the end, it's not meant for us! We're overhearers, not interlocutors. We're listeners-in, not conversation-partners. To our credit, we've always understood that. It's why we're popular with thinkers, W. says.

We don't have ideas, and we don't pretend to! In the end, we demand nothing, we ask for nothing. The lightness of our chatter (for we speak when our thinker is silent) is like the murmur of grasshoppers on a summer evening. The to-and-fro of our banter is like the trickling of a young stream: a backdrop, a kind of night against which the star of the idea can burn ever brighter.

In the final judgement, if we were not thinkers — if we never had an idea of our own — then neither did we *hinder* thought. We were not its enemies. *They were not enemies of thought:* isn't that what they might write on our tombstones?

Ah, but there are no thinkers with us today, as we stroll around the lake at Leazes Park. We've been thrown back on ourselves, once again! Thrown back: not upon thought and the development of thought, but upon the babble of non-thought, with no real thinker in sight.

'Did you bring some Schnapps?', W. asks. I brought some Schnapps. — 'Is it chilled?' It's straight from the freezer, I tell him, as the Danes would serve it.

Aalborg akavit, for our picnic. Did Kierkegaard drink Aalborg akavit?, W. wonders. Undoubtedly! Kierkegaard would certainly have drunk it in his early years, his pagan years, W. says. He probably drank himself blind on Aalborg akavit before his return to his faith, just as we must drink ourselves blind on Aalborg akavit, we who are lacking in faith, in Kierkegaard's faith.

And did I bring the herrings? Yes, I brought the herrings, and a disc-shaped packet of crispbread, and some cod roe sandwich paste from the grocery in *Ikea*. And we have some ryebread, too. — 'Good', W. says, 'we're well prepared'. To *think* like a Dane, you need to *eat and drink* like a Dane, we agree.

We're *method thinkers*, we've decided. A bit like method actors. It's a question of immersing ourselves in what we study. Of plunging into it. We have to become more Kierkegaardian than Kierkegaard, W. says. More Danish than the melancholy Dane!

It's like reverse engineering, W. says. We begin with the finished product, i.e., the complete works of Kierkegaard in the Hong and Hong edition, and we work our way back to the mind of the thinker who produced them. But not only to the mind! To the *cultural world* of the thinker; in this case, to the cultural world of nineteenth century Denmark. And to the *physiognomy* of the thinker; in this case, a melancholy disposition, a heaviness of the soul. We must move from the outward to the inward, W. says. Only then, having reached the secret centre of the work, having come to its *engine room* so to speak, might we work our way back out again.

Of course, one mustn't start reading too soon, W. is adamant about that. One mustn't simply *devour an oeuvre*, tempting as it may be, the many-coloured spines of Kierkegaard's works in the Hong and Hong edition, lined up on my windowsill, as inviting as boiled sweets.

One cannot just begin at page one, and then read one's way to the end, W. says. There must be a kind of pause before reading, a dwelling in the space opened by the *fact* of Kierkegaard, by the *fact* of his writing, by the *fact* that he lived.

That Kierkegaard wrote: we should pause before that, mulling it over, W. says. *That Kierkegaard was at all*: we must pause before that, too. And that *we* exist at all, in our stupidity: ah, that's what's unbearable, W. says. The fact that, despite our best intentions, we'll never be able to understand a word of Kierkegaard.

What is the connection between Kierkegaard and capitalism?: that's our question, W. says. What does Kierkegaard tell us about the *despair* of capitalism? These are the questions that must accompany us on our lecture tour of Britain, of the doomed universities of Great Britain.

The train south. County Durham. Open fields. Hamlets nestled into the countryside.

W. speaks of his Canadian boyhood. Things seemed so simple then, among the forests and the lakes! His body and soul were one. He lived in fellowship and harmony with the world. He would never have needed to think, had his family not returned to Britain, W. says. Had they not *fallen to earth* in this ridiculous country. He would have had nothing to think against. To read against!

Wasn't it in Britain that his first intellectual adventures began? Wasn't it here that he was dazzled by the bright orange dust-jackets of the Schocken edition of Kafka? The Canadian has no need for Kafka, W. says. A Canadian Kafka-reader is a contradiction in terms!

W. tells me the latest research on *cow intelligence*. Brighter cows *network*, W. says — they go from cow to cow, nuzzling their fellows, licking them, reminding them that they exist. Soon they become sought after, even dominant. The other cows rush to meet them. More stupid cows never network, never approach their fellows, W. says. Eventually, all the other cows stand with their backs to them. — 'Is there a lesson here, do you think?'

I can't feign friendliness, W. says. I can't feign *interest*. In the end, the art of conversation is entirely alien to me, W. says. The art of greeting people. When he did try to teach me, it led to disaster. I bellowed. *Hello!*, I cried in my loudest voice. — 'You scare people'.

Sometimes, the power to speak deserts me altogether, W. says, and the other person has to guess what I want to say. It invariably happens when things are most urgent, and I need to be most succinct. There's a great stuttering and stammering. A great foaming at the mouth. — 'You can't get a word out, can you?' W. has to intervene in such situations. 'Gesture!', he says. 'Mime! What is it? More food? Something else to drink?'

Still heading south.

He can see my lips moving as I read, W. says. It's not a good sign in a scholar. And I read too *quickly*! I read like a maniac!

You have to *linger* over the page, W. says. You have to *annotate* as you read. Write notes!

I have no real idea *how* to read, W. says. No idea how to *approach* the oeuvre of a great thinker, head on, as he does, reading the primary text in the original, line by line, looking up difficult words in a dictionary. I have no sense that I should come at an oeuvre from *upstream*, as it were, gaining a knowledge of the tradition of which it is a part, of the thinkers that influenced its author. I have no awareness of the importance of *context*, of the centrality of *history*.

I rely on secondary commentaries, on idiot's guides, W. says. In the end, I am only a *ransacker* of books, a kind of reader-marauder. My reading is a great pillaging, as if by a Viking raiding party.

This has to be our last lecture tour, W. says. This has to be the last time, the last dog and pony show. Why do we bother? What do we have to say to others? To *teach*?

W. feels the hatred of past generations, he says. Of our ancestors who thought something good might come out of their struggles. Of our forebears who lived and died in the hope that life in this world might be bettered. We've betrayed them!, W. says. We've stamped on their dreams!

And W. feels the hatred of our descendants, of the ones who are not yet born. We've stolen their hope, W. says. The very *grounds* of their hope. We've stolen their *world*! He hears their cries, W. says. He hears their wailing. They're not yet born; they've yet to appear on their scorched and burning earth: but he can feel their hatred even now.

W. wants to see how it all ends, he says. He wants to see how it will all turn out. But this *is* how it ends: him on a train, travelling with an idiot. This *is* how it will all turn out...

'*The true and only virtue is to hate ourselves*', W. says, reading from his notebook. To hate ourselves: what a task! He'll begin with me, W. says. With hating me. Then he'll move on to hating what I've made him become. What I've been responsible for. Then — the last step — he will have to hate himself without reference to me at all.

This step, for him, will be the most difficult. He can hardly remember what he was like without me! He has no idea what he might have been, what he might have achieved. I arrived too early in his life. The blow was fatal.

It's a relief, of course, W. says. He can blame me for everything. It's all my fault, his failure, his inability to think! In fact, that's probably why he hangs out with me, W. says: to have a living excuse for his failure, his inability to think.

The Thames Valley. Villas on the hillside. Barges on the river. Stations flashing by.

W. fell into a four-week depression when he received his letter of redundancy, he says. Day after day, he stared out of the window, like the guy in the opening scene of Tarr's *Damnation*. The contingency of it all! His manager had put his name forward to be sacked. That was it. The cursor had blinked over his name. And he received his letter: '*We'd like to take this opportunity to thank you for your years of service...*' But it might have happened otherwise. His manager might have selected someone else for redundancy. The cursor might have blinked over a name other than his.

We live insignificant lives, W. says. We live like ants. Like cockroaches. He'd give anything to believe in *fate*, like the ancient Greeks, W. says. Or to believe that God *willed* our sufferings. That our sufferings matter: that's what Kierkegaard thought, isn't it?, W. says. He remembers the line from Kierkegaard that he copied into his notebook: '*Suffering teaches us the great lesson of dying to the world, and to worldiness*'.

Does the contingency of *my* suffering bother *me*?, W. wonders. He knows about my years of *un*employment and *under*employment, W. says. He knows I've lived my life in a succession of rooms, each more squalid than the last. He knows I've lived my life *beneath the pavement*.

But W. wonders whether I ever really *experienced* my despair, he says. I've never grasped my despair in its philosophical dimension, W. says. In its *political* dimension. I've never asked myself about the *conditions* of my despair, W. says. About the forces that *constitute* it. I've never asked myself about the *whole*, the *totality*, the *order of things*. I've never railed against the haphazard nature of my despair. The fact that things *could have been otherwise*.

He'd like to think that our despair *calls* us, W. says. That it *singles us out*. That despair is like a beacon shining upon us, calling us to a new destiny. That despair, in some sense, is like the *voice of God*, summoning us to our vocation. *Here I am*: that was Moses's response, when God spoke to him from the burning bush. Here I am, who would pledge himself in service to you.

And God told Moses that He knew of the pain of his people. That He knew of their tribulations, and had heard their outcry. — '*And I have come down to rescue you from the land of Egypt and to bring you up to a good and spacious land, to a land flowing with milk and honey*'.

Moses' despair gave way to a divinely appointed task, W. says. Despair blossomed into hope. Will the same thing happen to us?, W. wonders. Will *our* despair blossom into hope? Are *we* heading to the land of milk and honey?

I knew Reading would appal him, I tell W. The town itself is just like any other town, the usual shops, the usual new developments along the river. Except that it's *more* like any other town than any other town. And here in the suburbs, the extent of its horror becomes very clear.

Blank-box executive homes, five to a plot. '70s semis with barn-sized extensions. Driveways packed with Land Rovers and 4X4s... Mock Tudor houses... Mock Georgian ones, with pebbledash rendering and plastic windows. Labyrinthine estates with roads named after flowers, after colours, after days of the week. Minor roads, thick with cars. Cars and car-parks and front gardens tarmacked over and covered in cars...

There are older streets, too, with great canopying trees. Villas subdivided into flats. Victorian houses with pattern-tiled paths and iron railings. The sun flashing on conservatory glass. And private schools, with their girls in boaters, with their boys in caps and blazers, and mothers at their gates in sparkling jeeps. W. is overwhelmed by class hatred, he says. He recites the names of Marxist revolutionaries to calm himself down...

The Reading yuppies are raising their young to be more rapacious than they are, W. says. More grasping than they are. They're treating them to babyccinos in chi-chi cafés.

They're sending them to the best schools. And one day, they'll get work experience and internships for them. One day, the children will find work in the corporations of Reading, and the children will start their careers in the suburbs of Reading. And the whole cycle will begin again...

Only the capitalism-hardened can survive here, W. says. Only self-marketers and self-advertisers. Only those who perform PR for their own souls...

As for everyone else?: Suicide!, W. says. Exile! Despair! Terrible depressions! Derangements of the spirit! Half of the Reading young are starving themselves in darkness, W. says. Half of them are slicing up their arms in secret. Half of them think of death and only death. Half of them pray for the apocalypse.

The suburbs are so *thick* in Reading, W. says. So *condensed*. They're almost real. They've almost managed to pass themselves off as reality.

W. reminds me of Philip K. Dick's gnostic vision. For Dick, the world as we see it is a stage-set. It's unreal. History ended in AD70, when the Romans sacked Jerusalem, and destroyed the Temple. For Dick, this horror has never stopped happening, W. says. What we know as history is an illusion overlain on perpetual injustice. Jerusalem is eternally being sacked. The Temple is eternally being destroyed.

In Reading, history ended in the 1980s, W. says. In Reading, the council houses are eternally being sold off. Housing estates are eternally being built. Golf courses are eternally opening up. The corporations are eternally moving in...

Yew trees. A grassy expanse. Reading University campus.

To think there's a university in the midst of it all, W. says. To think there's a campus on the edge of such a town, like a mall or a leisure complex. Like a DIY superstore...

And to think there's a *department of philosophy* in the midst of it all, W. says. To think there's some pretence at *thinking* in Reading.

Welcome packs. Book flyers and publishers' catalogues. A timetable of parallel sessions, and a booklet of presentation abstracts. Haven't we vowed never to attend this kind of thing again?, W. says, fixing on his nametag.

Professors like great walruses, in elasticated trousers. Swarms of young lecturers, looking to impress. Looking to *network*! Tweed everywhere. Wall-to-wall tweed. Tweed jackets and trousers. Tweed in the head!

We need a panic room, W says. A *war* room! And we need a general strategy. In the meantime... — 'Keep your head down. Talk to no one!'

W. recognises the plenary speaker as an ally. Young academics throng around him. — 'He's drowning!', W. says. 'We can't just leave him there!'

In the pub, we wait for our plates of sausage and mash. — 'You know they hate you', W. says to the plenary speaker. 'They hate us, God knows, and they hate you, too'. — 'Who hates me?', the plenary speaker asks. — 'Everyone. Everyone here', W. says. — '*I* don't think they hate me', the plenary speaker says. — 'They do! They hate us, and they *really* hate you'.

'They hate thought!, W. insists. 'Don't you see? They hate thought, and want to drive all thought away!' — 'Why did they invite me, then?', the plenary speaker wonders. It's a mystery, we agree. Perhaps there's still some instinct among the Reading philosophers concerning what they lack, W. speculates. Perhaps they feel some residual *shame* about their inability to think.

He feels shame, W. tells the plenary speaker. He's been trying to teach *me* the meaning of shame, he says. But how can you teach a grown man shame? If only W. had known me as a child, what I might have been! Give us a child till the age of seven, and he'll be ours for life: that's the Jesuits, W. says. Give us a fully grown adult idiot, and he'll be our scourge for life: that's what he's learnt, W. says.

Sausages and mash arrive on big oval plates. It looks disgusting, we agree, but what can you expect for £3.95? Eat up!, we urge our speaker. He needs to keep up his strength! After all, very soon he'll have to go back to the conference! We'll protect him, we tell the plenary speaker. We'll flank him like the president's secret service bodyguards. We'll keep our sunglasses on and speak into earpieces. — 'The package is in the building', we'll say. 'The package is about to give his presentation'.

Fog descends as we head back to the campus. It's as thick as the cloud on Mount Sinai, when Moses went up to meet God, W. says. Moses descended with the Tablets of Law, W. says — what will *we* bring back with us?

We're hopelessly lost. The plenary speaker's worried. What about the conference meal? He's supposed to be sitting at the high table. — 'Never mind the high table!', W. says. The plenary speaker's too full of sausage and mash to be able to eat anything else, for one thing. — 'You've a real appetite!', W. says to him, impressed.

It's a verdant campus, we agree. Very lush. The Thames Valley's known for its humidity. It's very bad for asthmatics. I developed asthma as a child, I've told W. that. And eczema. — 'And lice', W. says.

In the thick darkness: that's where God was waiting for Moses, W. says. In the thick darkness: that's how God appears to the mystic, Gregory of Nyssa said. The mystic receives a *dark vision* of God. But what do we see? Not God, at any rate. Barely even each other! It's a real *pea-souper*, we agree, speaking like the commoners in *Brief Encounter*. Cor blimey, guv'nor.

The plenary speaker feels unwell. Our ally feels unwell! What have we done to him?, we wonder. How can we make reparation?

We tell him of our Kierkegaard project, our collaborative endeavour, for which we are compiling voluminous notes. We tell him about the intimate link we expect to discover between Kierkegaard and contemporary capitalism; about the Danish philosopher's despair and *our* despair.

The plenary speaker is silent. We need to say something else! Religion! What does our speaker think about religion?,

W. asks. Does he, like W., have a sense of the *urgency* of the question of religion? The plenary speaker says he has no particular thoughts about religion. What about despair, then? What does he think about despair?

Silence again. Do we drink?, the plenary speaker asks us. He drinks, he says. He drinks every night. *Do* we drink?: we muse. Of course we drink! Whatever can he mean, *Do we drink!?* What kind of question is that? What are we being asked? *Do* we drink?, we wonder. Have we ever drunk? Ah, but what do we know of drinking, and what could we know? And about despair, about religion: what could we know about those topics, either?

The plenary speaker falls back into silence. — 'Marx and Kierkegaard', W. says finally. 'We intend to think the conjunction of Marx and Kierkegaard. They were born in the same year, you know'.

The plenary speaker's feeling really ill now. The fog's thickening. We need to stay close! Keep a head count! And it's darkening, too. Are we really going to meet our God? Do you think we'll receive the Tablets of Law? — 'Go on, say something profound', W. says to the plenary speaker.

The slow train to London.

'We're in the suburbs of a suburb', W. says. 'In the suburbs of a suburb of a suburb...'

I point out my old school as we pass. I had the worst of schooling, I tell W. No one knew anything: we didn't know anything; our teachers didn't know anything. The blind led the blind. The blind stabbed out the eyes of the sighted. *They stabbed out our eyes*, I tell W.

I point out the warehouse where I worked as a contractor when I left school. It was the worst of jobs, I tell W. No one spoke to anyone else. Nothing meant anything. Our jobs were a mockery of jobs. Companies employed us half-time, quarter-time, changing our hours week by week. Labour flexibility, they called it. Underemployment, that's what *we* called it.

There are still bits of countryside left behind by the suburbs, we notice from the train. Forlorn horses in tiny fields. Rabbits hopping across a golf course. Rats crawling along a wall by the sewage treatment works.

W. pictures me as a teenager, cycling out to every green patch I could find on the map. He pictures me making my way through fir plantations to the scrap of woodland fenced off by the Ministry of Defence, where solders used to come to train for future wars. He pictures me listening out for artillery fire, and hearing nothing but the wind in the trees and birds singing.

Like everyone else, I went to work in the hi-tech industrial estate. W. pictures me heading home from work, past the fenced-off patches of land between the company buildings of Winnersh Triangle. He pictures me looking over long puddles in the mud, after the gypsies had churned up the grass with their caravans. This was all that was left of the wilderness! All that was left of unused space!

'So you went north', W. says. I went north. — 'Of course you did, where else were you to go?' To the north, the very opposite of the suburban south! To the north, of decaying industry and terminal rustzones! To the north, of canal towpaths and broken girders! To the north of rain, eternal rain!

I went to Manchester, the city of eternal blight. I went to study in the city of mass unemployment and mass misery. I went to study philosophy in a city that had been left to fall apart like a Russian space station.

And did I *find my people?*, W. says, knowing the answer. Did the Mancunians welcome me as *one of their own*? No! — muggers held knives to my throat. Junkies trailed after me asking me for money.

I found a cheap bedsit next to the curry house extractor fans, didn't I?, W. says. There's a crack in the wall, I told the landlord, when he showed me the room. — 'A crack in the wall, yes', he said, and smiled. I could hardly breathe for cold and curry, but I took the room nonetheless, because it cost nothing and I had nothing. — 'You were born for squalor', W. says.

'Staines — what a name for a town!', W. says. And, a little later, 'Egham — it's unbearable!'

This is *suicide country*, W. says. He'd top himself if he lived here. He'd either top himself, or think some great thought, W. says.

To think against the suburbs. To think in the suburbs, hating the suburbs. What pressure of thinking you could build up! What a head of steam! — 'But it didn't work for you, did it?'

He sees why, W. says. The suburbs only gave me fear — the fear of falling back into the suburbs. The fear of crash-landing here, where I grew up. That's why I've flung myself into administration, W. says. That's why I've tried to lodge myself in the administrative work of the university, like a tick in an armpit. — 'But they'll find you in the end', W. says. 'They'll smoke you out and recapture you. And there you'll be, coughing in the suburban sun...'

We speculate about the *lost geniuses of the suburbs*. Bracknell's secret Rilke (Coetzee lived in Bracknell, W. says)... Martin Heron's hidden Leibniz (W.: 'Martin Heron!?'). And Sunningdale's own Solomon Maimon, drunk in *Tesco's* carpark...

You'd have to go on the sick, if you lived in the suburbs, W. says. You'd have to stay unemployed, wandering the streets with the early-retired and the mothers pushing buggies. And you'd go mad from isolation. You'd go off your head. And then you'd top yourself.

Why do I always bring *Hello!* magazine with me on our train journeys?, W. wonders. Why do I insist on leaving it in his study when I come to stay?

'Who are all these people?', he wants to ask me, when he sees me reading. 'Why do they matter to you?' Because they *do* matter to me, that much is clear, W. says. The *way* I read. The *way* I nod my head over the glossy pages, like a Jew over the Talmud, W. says. He sees, as at no other time, a look of absolute seriousness on my face. There it is: an intensity of focus that only the Husserl archives could warrant.

'What are you looking for?', W. says. What, in Oscar dresses and airbrushed actresses? What, in the photospreads of Queen Rania of Jordan?

In the end, I admire the great philosophers only as I admire the celebrities in my gossip magazines. Their brilliance is only the equivalent of a celebrity's beauty; their integrity only the fervour of an ingénue's rise to fame. My stupidity places them at an infinite and glamorous remove.

It's different with him, W. says. He's that little bit cleverer than me, that little bit farther ahead, and it's enough that his non-intelligence, unlike mine, is commensurable with real intelligence; his non-integrity, with real integrity. At least he has the *glimmerings* of the faith of a Rosenzweig, a Weil and a Kierkegaard, W. says. At least he has an *idea* of belief.

When he writes of them, he leaves the great thinkers

intact in their magnificence. They remain remote and brilliant in the sky of thought. But when *I* write of them? I make others *doubt*, W. says. I make others *despair*. Are Rosenzweig, Weil and Kierkegaard really so worthwhile if *Lars* is writing on them?, people ask themselves. Can they really be so great if *Lars* is thinking about them?

He needs a tranquiliser gun, W. says, with a dart strong enough to bring down an elephant. How else is he going to stop me rampaging through philosophy, tearing up everything with my tusks?

That I write on Western philosophy is really the *destruction* of Western philosophy, W. says. That I write on religious ideas is really the *destruction* of all religious ideas. And that I pretend to think is really the *destruction* of thought, affecting all thinkers, everywhere.

Schelling, Feuerbach... no one's safe when I begin to think. Maimon, Nicholas of Cusa... Is there anyone who might be saved?

A rumbling through the heavens: Lars is writing one of his commentaries! Angels' cries: Lars is defiling Rosenzweig! And Weil! And Kierkegaard — what's Lars going to do with him?

No one reads a line *he* writes, W. says. What *he* writes is of no significance at all. But when *I* write — when I publish my reflections, if he can call it publishing, if he can call them reflections — he wants to clasp the entire oeuvres of Bataille, Weil and Kierkegaard to his breast, W. says. He wants to build a big wall around the library and all libraries, posting sentries to shoot me on sight. But he knows, like the Red

Death of Poe's story, that I'm in there already, that my reading is eating away at those oeuvres like cancer.

Twickenham. Putney. And Clapham Junction, where the track braids together with a myriad of others, and trains like ours run a parallel course.

My life in Manchester, in old Manchester, before the regeneration. What was I reading in my bedsit by the curry house extractor fans?, W. wonders. What, as cold air poured into my room from the crack in the wall? Kafka, of course. Kafka, spuriously.

W. read Kafka as he travelled through Europe, as he surveyed the European scene from his train window. He read about the Austro-Hungarian empire and its collapse, as the train passed through Freiburg, and about the generation of German Jews in its final hour, as he arrived in Strasbourg.

As his train crossed the Alps, W. read about Benjamin and Scholem who, making constant reference to Kafka, discussed the fine line between religion and nihilism in their letters. In a café in Berne, W. read of their attempt to develop, each in their own way, a kind of *anarcho-messianism*, an *apocalyptic antipolitics*, and their discussion about whether the coming of the Messiah meant the *dissolution* of the Law or its *fulfilment*.

And me — what was I reading to contextualise my Kafka studies? What, as I wandered through the university library?

But I had no idea of Kafka's milieu. To me, Kafka was only a meteor who had arrived from nowhere.

It was Kafka who led me from the south to the north, W. knows that. It was Kafka who led me into the university. Before Kafka, there was my warehouse life. My life as a finder of UTLs, unable-to-locates, searching up and down the warehouse aisles.

I stumbled when I tried to convey it to W., when I tried to explain what Kafka revealed to me in my warehouse years. I spoke of the castle hill, veiled in mist and darkness, and of the buzzing and whistling on the telephone line. I spoke of the *illusory emptiness* into which K. looked up as he crossed the wooden bridge, and of his weariness, which made him collapse on the way to settle his business with the authorities. What was I getting at?, W. wonders. What was I trying to say?

The world around me was unreal, I told W. that. The warehouse was unreal. The suburbs in which I had grown up, and on which the warehouse had been built, were likewise unreal. Despair reveals the truth of the world: isn't that what was shown to me by Kafka? Suffering reveals the *nullity of things*.

I had a vision, I told W., he remembers. I saw the workers around me like rats in a rat-run. I saw the pristine buildings around me like rat-pens, like rat-mazes. Absurdity was doing experiments on us: that's what I saw, wasn't it? Madness had us caged in the suburbs like laboratory rats...

My soul was a UTL: isn't that what I saw? Life was an unable-to-locate, although no one seemed to know it but me.

The Castle made my life quiver like a compass needle. Things pointed in one direction: north! Out of the warehouse!

Out of the south! North: to where dereliction, like *The Castle*, revealed things in their truth! North: to where the destruction of the created order had worn through! To where *reality* had worn through!

Where have the homeless gone, who used to sleep under the bridge at Waterloo?, W. wonders. Doubtless, they were blasted awake by hoses at three or four in the morning. Doubtless they were *moved on* by the new security guards, the private police of Capital...

We've seen them, in our home cities, of course: the *Business Improvement Officers*, in their fluorescent vests, walkie-talkies squawking. We've seen them patrolling the Newcastle streets in teams, ensuring a *clean and safe trading environment* by moving undesirables away. We've seen them safeguarding the *marketing and branding of the area* by breaking up groups of teenagers and moving on the homeless in Plymouth shopping malls.

There's to be no loitering in the privatised city centre (but there's nowhere to loiter). No sitting down (but there are no benches on which to sit down). There are to be no non-consumers in the new imperium. That's why the Business Improvement Officers are out with their hoses in the early hours of the morning. That's why they're keeping watch through CCTV for any *non-consumerist behaviour*.

Waterloo Bridge. The mighty Thames.

Bridges are offensive to the gods, W.'s read. They're the

symbol of hubris, of over-striving. Who would think themselves stronger than the currents and tides?

The gods of the river need to be appeased, W. says. The Greeks used to suspend animals over the river and then cut their throats. They used to throw live horses into the waters, or sacrifice them on the banks. The pagans had the tradition of sacrificing *children* to appease the river. W. shudders.

The Thames is full of all kinds of offerings: jewellery and figurines, spear-heads and battle axes, mutilated pagan deities, crucifixes with the head of Jesus removed, lying perfectly preserved in river-bottom silt...

Should we throw ourselves in?, we wonder, looking down at the restless, heaving water. Ah, but the river wouldn't want us. We would appease the wrath of no god, we who are neither innocent, like children, nor full of life, like horses. We'd be pulled up from the waves, the polluted water pumped from our stomachs. They'd slap us round the face. *Wake up! Wake up!* And W.'s eyes would open and see me. And he'd retch up the black river water from the bottom of his lungs.

Somerset House. The vast courtyard. Pavilions and porticos. Posh people eating lunch in the sun. He knows I didn't want to come here, W. says. He can see that I am uncomfortable in such grand surroundings. The working class are only happy in squalor. But W. wouldn't be deterred from going to Somerset House. He wanted to see the fountain, he says. He wanted to see the jets of water rising and falling. And he wanted to see me caper among those jets like an idiot child.

The bottle of wine that we ordered arrives, with two glasses. — 'To us!', toasts W. To idiocy!, I toast. How do I think our lecture tour is going?, W. asks. Are we coming through with our reputations intact? Our dignity? Have we gained in stature in the eyes of our contemporaries? Ah, there's no need to answer.

This is our last tour, W. says. He feels that strongly. Something's going to happen. Something's about to happen... Why does he feel such a sense of dread?

In his dreams, we're on the beach, and the sea's out, sucked out, as it is before a great wave comes, W. says. But only he knows the tsunami's coming. Only he knows, and no one will listen to him. And there I am, inflatable around my midriff, running down the beach towards the sea...

There's nothing left for us, W. says. Nothing left to

do except drink and dance. He'll drink, W. says, and I'll dance. — 'Go on, fat boy, dance!'

In these times, we should be cultivating an *aristocratic detachment*, W. says. We should retire from the fray like Roman Stoics, holing up on our country estates while the empire crumbles... — 'But we haven't got country estates!', W. says. We haven't.

Should we order another bottle? — 'Of course we should!' W. learned it from Debord, from Bacon: the art of luxurious dining at the end of times. He's read of Debord, in his later years, in his luxurious apartment on the rue du Bac, spending whole days planning elaborate meals and choosing fine wines. He was a *'warrior at rest'*, Debord said of himself. He'd *'lain down his arms'*, he'd had enough. *'This century does not like truth, generosity, grandeur'*, Debord wrote. And Bacon left painting behind in 1935, and gave himself over to champagne, promiscuity and gambling. To a *'furious frivolity'*, as his biographer puts it, to living a *'grand style of existence...'*

Let's order some sandwiches, too, we agree.

Upstairs in *Foyles*, looking through the philosophy books.

'Do you think they'll have our books here?', W. asks, knowing the answer. 'Of course not!' His book went out of print as soon as it was published. *Before* it was published! His publisher went bust. And my books — my so-called books — appeared in the most obscure of imprints, by the most obscure of presses, at a price affordable only by the most prosperous libraries. Our books will have no effect whatsoever! They'll have no readers!

Ah, but he still believes, deep in his heart, that our collaboration might lead to something great, W. says. That's what keeps him going, even if all the evidence is to the contrary. Why can't I see it? Why have I given up on him? On *us*?

'When are you going to take philosophy seriously?', W. says. 'You haven't read anything in years. Are you *retiring* from philosophy?', he asks. 'Have you given up?' I haven't, I tell him. — 'Then why don't you *write* some philosophy? You have to *externalise* yourself. You have to *experience* your shortcomings'.

I show W. a book of photos of Deleuze and Guattari from the '70s, with their flares and long hair. Look at them! They were having a good time! — 'They had ideas', W. says. 'They were changing the world'.

The Idiot's Guide to Deleuze… Deleuze for the Simple… Deleuze as Pabulum, in the *Pre-chewed Philosophy* series, and *Deleuze in Bullet Points* in the *Lowest Common Denominator* series. *Ninny Deleuze*, in the *Reducing Everything to Common Sense* series. *Deleuze Vivisected*, in the *Yet More Books Explaining Deleuze* series… — 'Do you think there are enough introductory books to Deleuze?', W. asks. But Deleuze is *hard*, I point out. Deleuze *is* hard, W. says. Philosophy is hard! It shouldn't be made any easier!

W. carried Deleuze's *Logic of Sense* around in his man bag for a month, he says. He never understood a word of it. The criterion for a book of worth is: does it make you think more, W. says. Did the *Logic of Sense* make him think more?, I ask him. It made him experience his idiocy in a new way, which is a very valuable thing, W. says.

Idiocy isn't one thing, W. says. There are *kinds* of idiocy. *Tones* of idiocy. His *Deleuzian* idiocy is very different from his *Rosenzweigian* idiocy, W. says. From his *Kierkegaardian* idiocy! He experiences the limits of thought differently with every philosopher he reads! And isn't that the only reason to read, W. says: to experience your limits anew? To experience your *idiocy*?

W. reads me a passage from an encyclopaedia entry on Hermann Cohen:

> *In Cohen's hands, this historical orientation contributes in no small part to other aspects of his writing that none of his readers can fail to notice: its obscurity, repetition, and sometimes unnecessary length.*

Don't they understand that Cohen should be *praised* for his style?, W. says. That the philosopher, *least of all*, is obliged to be clear? The philosopher *shouldn't* understand what he's doing, W. says. He *shouldn't* know where his thought is going; and nor should his readers.

W. finds the book for which I wrote a blurb: Jean-Luc Nancy's *Listening*. — 'Ah, the high point of your worldly renown', W. says. 'Did Jean-Luc Nancy ask for you personally?', W. asks. 'Did he esteem your amazing Blanchot scholarship?'

W. reads the blurb: '*sense resounds beyond significance in the experience of listening*'. I'm *aping* Nancy, W. says. Aping his style. There's nothing more grotesque than a British person aping the style of a French thinker, W. says.

W. remembers my attempt to *become Blanchot*. It was hilarious. I was the least likely Blanchotian. The Blanchotian with the least French. With the least *idea* of France. The only Blanchotian who'd never *been* to France. Who had never ridden the Paris Métro. Who had never eaten a Parisian crêpe.

Blanchotian scholars should at least be thin, as Blanchot was thin, W. says. They should at least be unwell — as Blanchot was unwell. And they should wear black, W. says. Not some blousy shirt with great flowers. Not grimy pantaloons, billowing like great sails.

Westminster Abbey. The Houses of Parliament. Whitehall, and then Downing Street, seen through the iron grille of the gate.

W. thinks he has *London sickness*, he says, remembering the title of one of Blanchot's essays. At first, he's awed at the sights, then bored, then depressed. There are too many spectacles! And spectacles make us into spectators, nothing more! I am to lead him somewhere calm, W. says, as Antigone led the blinded Oedipus.

London Aquarium embraces us with its darkness. Tell him all I know, W. says. It's one of my odd corners of knowledge: aquatic life, he says. And sometimes, he finds it soothing to be told things. He likes facts to wash over him. Facts about fish, for example. Facts about ocean currents and migratory patterns.

W. remembers my great *fish lectures* at the aquarium in Plymouth. He remembers my telling him about the shoaling behaviour of turbot and Dover sole, and about their favoured habitats and mating habits.

Plymouth's is a *local* aquarium, I told W. I appreciated that, and made W. appreciate it, too. It wasn't about the colourful marine fish that you can see anywhere. It wasn't all clown fish and anemones. It was about Plymouth — the aquatic life of Plymouth and its environs, I said, over our plates of freshly caught turbot and Dover sole in *Platters*.

London Aquarium isn't a local aquarium, I tell W. It isn't content to display dogfish and eels. It's a *prestige* aquarium, I say, which makes things entirely different. It's a *capital city* aquarium...

I soothe him with my chatter, W. says. And the darkness of the aquarium makes him think he's sinking underground. That he's lying down and giving up, and rotting in the humus with all the dead of London.

W. has no understanding of Danish *pathos*, he says. He doesn't understand the *mood* of Denmark.

Tungsind: that's the one Danish word he has to understand, haven't I told him that? *Tungsind*: Danish melancholy. Nineteenth century Danish melancholy. Isn't that what Kierkegaard said he suffered from? Isn't that what had been passed down to him from his father? And hasn't it been passed down to *all* Danes, even though Denmark is supposed to be the happiest country in Europe?

It's why the Danes are such bad drunks, W. says. Danes show themselves at their worst when they drink. Tolerance, openness and liberal-mindedness go out of the window. Danish happiness is thrown out of the window. Danes become Vikings again, when they drink, W. says. But *defeated* Vikings, *brooding* Vikings who have lost all their fire, if not all their anger. The drunk Dane is full of a *weary* rage, a *resentful* ire. He knows, W. says: he sees it in me. — 'You can be so *cruel*. So *vicious*'.

Has my stalker followed us to London? — 'You do still have a stalker, don't you?' I do. — 'He's still following you about?' He is. He's always in the shadows, I tell W. He'll appear somewhere, when we least expect him. — 'It's going to end

59

in a stabbing', W. says. He's sure of it. 'Someone's going to stab you'.

I bring them on myself, W. says, the nutters and the weirdoes. What draws them to me, my mad men and women? Why am I the one they pick out from the crowd? Because they do pick me out. They follow me, buttonhole me, write incessant emails to me; he knows that. He's met them; they're terrifying.

More terrifying still is his role in all this, W. says. Is he a nutter? A weirdo? The worst of nutters, the worst of weirdoes, I tell him, which terrifies him all the more.

The Isle of Dogs. This is where suicides used to wash up, W. says. And this is where they'll wash up again, at the feet of the steel and glass buildings of Canary Wharf and its neighbours, where the financial services industry has its hub. This is it, the capital of the capital, W. says. We've found it: the real centre of London, with its great towers. We've found the centre, unashamed of its symbols of power and wealth...

There is a sublimity to Capital, a deathly beauty, we agree. It commands awe, like a starry sky. We could be in Shanghai, we agree. In Dubai...

Capitalism, unashamed of itself. Money, unashamed, coming into the open. A new day has begun. Capitalism is natural and eternal and unabashed...

We're at the beginning of a new age, W. says. A gleaming age. A steel-and-windows age. And there will come the men and women of the new age, taller than us, with bright eyes and white teeth. Taller, sleeker, with broader skill-sets.

And what will our role be, in the new age? What will happen to us, in the *new university*? Will we become *learning facilitators*, taking our students through the Microsoft philosophy package? Will we become *virtual guides* in the *Philosophy-World*™ learning environment?

Will we become *puppets of Capital*, teaching that our Britain is the best possible Britain, that history could only have led to our neoliberal present? Will we teach that all philosophers — even those most opposed to capitalism — are really *capitalist philosophers*, and that capitalism really is the truth of all things, that it was waiting there all along for us to catch up? Will we teach that all thoughts — even anticapitalist thoughts — are ultimately *thoughts of capitalism*, that every idea, in essence, is a *capitalist idea*?

We'll be drinking, W. says. Drinking and weeping by the side of the Thames.

These are the people who rule the world, we muse, as we stand among the commuters on the Docklands light railway. These are the eagles with outspread wings, riding the thermals of international capitalism. These are the eagles immune from it all, from the destruction of the world, and from the suicides that wash up against the towers...

W. reads out his favourite passage from Kraznahorkai, with great vehemence:

> *They have ruined everything they've managed to get*
> *their hands on. They've managed to get their hands*
> *on everything, ruined everything — seized it, ruined*
> *it, and carried on in this way until they have achieved*
> *complete victory, so that it is one long triumphal*
> *march of seizing and ruining...*

They *have* ruined everything, W. whispers, looking round at the commuters. They *are* destroying the world.

Double red lines along the road. Double yellow lines, those we understand, but double *red* ones? — 'Have you ever seen such a thing?', W. says. It must be because of the terrible volume of traffic, we agree. It must be because of the ceaseless procession of cars and vans.

How crowded the city is! How cramped, with its narrow pavements, and dead-eyed Londoners pushing you onto the street. There's no space to *breathe!* The dust, the terrible dust! We're choking! We're dying here!

W. is panicking. I sing snatches of our song to soothe him: '*Hey, little W....*' He sings along, still distraught.

W. has *London plague*, he says. He needs to *leave the capital!* We're men of the provinces, W. says. We're men of the periphery. But perhaps we might escape London *in London,* W. says. Perhaps we might escape into London's periphery.

That's what the Situationists sought in Paris, W. says. Human freedom, in urban form. A '*transformed cartography*' — that's what they called it. Wasn't that what they looked for in their *dérives*, their drifts: the utopia hidden in the city?

Debord and the others drifted for weeks around Paris, W. says. They passed through half-demolished houses and dossed down at night in public gardens, looking to escape '*alienation and reification writ in stone*'. They wandered through the caverns and tunnels of the quarries of Paris, and through the catacombs where the sign above the portal read, '*Stop! This is the empire of death*'. And they drank — how they drank! — to break their fetters, to usher in the reign of prodigality and glory: a true metropolitanism.

Some places drew them closer, some repelled them; they sank into some routes like fissures, following the cracks in the urban network. They drained into sinkholes and found havens in the drift, temporary stopping places: certain bars, certain quarters. But above all, they *moved*, and for months at a time. They moved, and the will to change life as it was moved with them. Life as it was, life as it is: they blazed through Paris like a trail of fire...

To move, to move. But where has our London drifting taken us?, W. wonders. He reads the sign. *The Trafalgar Tavern*. To the pub! Where else? Ah, he shouldn't have put me in charge of the drift, W. says.

W. is dreaming of the *Canadian city*, he says, over our pints. He's dreaming of a different kind of urbanism.

Can I imagine what Toronto is like?, W. asks. Can I *conceive* of Montreal, the jewel of Quebec? And Ottawa: what does Ottawa mean to me? He remembers Ottawa, W. says. He has loving memories of Ottawa.

Winnipeg. Edmonton. Yellowknife. Whitehorse...: W. whispers to himself as if incanting. He hasn't seen these cities, W. says. He can't imagine them...

The Canadian city is part of the wilderness, W. says; it includes it. To be inside the Canadian city is also to be inside the Canadian wilderness, he says mystically. The Canadian city is only a *fold* of the wilderness, a way of answering it, of continuing it in another medium.

The Canadian city is full of space, W. says. Its boulevards remember the ice-plains, its skyscrapers the gleaming summits among the mountains. Its windows flash back the aurora borealis to the sky. And its night-time darkness remembers that of the thick pine forests that cover the land.

And the Canadian city is full of *time*, W. says. Everyone has time. People — strangers — stop and talk to one another. The Canadians are a *patient* people, W. says. They're not to be rushed.

The Canadian city: that's where we would learn what patience was, W. says. That's where we would learn to take deep breaths and walk upright. — 'Even you! Even you might learn to take deep breaths and walk upright'.

And I might learn French, too, W. says. That's where he learned his French, in Canada, W. says. He grew up speaking French, Canadian French. The French of the Quebecois, he says. The French of the wilderness.

That's how you can calm a wilderness bear, W. says: by speaking to it in Quebecois French. That's how you can calm a wilderness wolf: by speaking softly, in a language full of space and time...

The hotel bar.

We need to work!, W. says. To think! But our minds are blank. We sit back in our chairs. We stretch our arms, then our legs. W. yawns and then I yawn. W. gets up and goes to the loo, and then I get up and go to the loo. Should we get something else to drink?, I wonder. Nothing else! We're here to *think*, not *drink*, W. says.

We pause to finish the dregs of our pints and look around the bar. Do they sell pork scratchings?, we wonder. W. sends me to the bar to ask about pork scratchings. — 'Fuck off and let me think'.

I come back with two more pints. W.'s still stuck. We rub our bellies with our hands and then pat the tops of our heads. Then we pat our bellies and rub the tops of our heads.

Inspiration! A thought's come to him, W. says. A thought prompted by Kierkegaard! — 'Take dictation! We refuse to confront the real object of our despair', W. says, 'We inflict despair on ourselves'. And then, 'We have to become *conscious* of our despair: that we are each both the *subject and the object* of our despair'.

Hasn't he always blamed *me* for his despair?, W. says. Hasn't he always assumed that it's *all my fault? If only I could be rid of Lars, that idiot,* he's said to himself. *If only I could ditch Lars somewhere...*

But what if it isn't all my fault? What if the fault lies with

W. himself? '*Despair is the gateway to the eternal*', W. reads from his copy of *The Sickness Unto Death*. '*Salvation will come, but only when we* choose *despair*': that's what Kierkegaard writes, W. says.

Has W. chosen despair: can he really say that?, he wonders. Has W. chosen *me*, the chief cause of his despair? Because that's what he must do, if he wants salvation. I, who am W.'s obstacle, am also his gateway. I, who block W.'s path, am also nothing other than his path.

It's not enough to say 'no' to me, W. says; he has to say 'yes', too. It was by embracing the leper he met on the highway that St Francis began his life as a mendicant. W. will have to embrace me, and then *be embraced*, not by me, who am not capable of embracing anyone, but by the Power that stands behind us both, testing us both, W. says.

Stuck again. W. looks into the air. He grinds his teeth. He clenches his fists, then unclenches them. Then he sees me looking at him. — 'You enjoy this, don't you?', W. says. I enjoy watching him *groping for thought*.

W. thinks of his other collaborators, over the years. Of others in whom he had placed his hopes. One by one, they were picked off by careerism, by laziness, by the temptations of *applied ethics* and the writing of introductory books.

Of course, it was really the *futility of thinking* that destroyed his collaborators, W. says. The lack of recognition. They expected their thought to be rewarded! They expected that the world would be interested in their *Denkwegs*, in their paths of thought. And when that didn't come? They sought recognition through other means.

He faces the opposite problem with me, W. says. I've long since thrown my arms around futility. I've long since driven my *Denkweg* into the quagmire of the blogosphere. The opposite of recognition: that's what I want, isn't it?, W. says. Public humiliation: that's what I crave...

W. googles *imbecile* and then *idiot*. He googles *enemy* and *betrayer*. W. googles *morbid obesity*. He googles *liposuction* and *gastric bands*. And then W. googles my website. — 'Let's see what rubbish you've written today'.

Ah, my internet delusion, W. says. My *blogospherical* delusion. Didn't I try to persuade him that the next great movement of thought would take place online, bypassing the conventional channels of thought? Didn't I tell him of *blogger-Lispectors* of the future, of *internet-Weils* to come?

W. was actually persuaded, he says. Or some part of him was. He actually thought something was happening, that something might come of it. We started our group blog, didn't we?, he says. Our collective. — 'And then what happened? Tell me. Start at the beginning'. A pause. 'You ruined it! You destroyed it!'

He remembers it all, W. says. I wrote like a maniac. Post after post, one after another. No one else in the collective had a chance! No one could get a word in! Logorrhoea: is that what I had? *Blogorrhoea*! I was a maniac of writing, W. says. I was a *Rasputin of prose*.

I wrote on the last wildernesses in the Home Counties. I wrote on life in the suburbs of the Thames Valley. I wrote on my beleaguered childhood. And I wrote of the damp invading my flat and of the rats beneath my flat. I wrote about the end of the world, without understanding that my writing was also part of the end of the world.

Occasionally, W. would put up one of his considered, reasonably-written posts, he says. Every now and then, after much thought, W. would put something up — a modest post, soberly written — supposing that, surrounded by my madness, his post might seem all the more reasonable. He thought his post might rise up, a calm island in a crazy ocean.

But that's not what happened, is it? His post was swamped! Everything he wrote was drowned! It was Atlantis all over again. That's when he learned that the internet was only a support network for my fantasies, W. says. That's when he learned that the blogosphere was invented for *people like me.*

W. reads me a passage from one of Debord's films:

It must be admitted that none of this is very clear. It is a completely typical drunken monologue, with its incomprehensible allusions and tiresome delivery. With its vain phrases that do not await response and its overbearing explanations. And its silences.

'That's how you should preface everything you write', W. says.

Greenwich, London. The boulevards of the Royal Naval College are wide and calm, and we wander them like aristocrats. This is where they'll set up base after the revolution, we agree. This is where we'll be tried and executed by the new revolutionary order... — *'It was all his fault!'*, W. will cry as they raise the blade of the guillotine above our necks. *'Him — blame him!'* And our heads will shoot out thirty feet over the crowds...

Ah, what kind of revolutionaries would we make?, W. says. Who would lead who to the scaffold? Would I be the Robespierre to his Danton, sending him to his death? Or would it be the other way round?

W. can see them now, meeting together for the last time, two old friends, soon to be estranged: Danton dishevelled as usual, half drunk as usual; and Robespierre in his sky-blue cloak, with his immaculately powdered wig, believing himself to embody the revolution, and defending the murder of sixteen thousand people under the guillotine.

'What of those among the dead who are innocent?', Danton asked his friend, in his *basso profundo* voice. — *'I suppose that a man of your moral principles would not think that anyone deserved punishment'*, said Robespierre. Danton's reply was quick: *'And I suppose that you would be annoyed if no one did'*.

Robespierre rose and left, his cape sweeping about him. Danton wept bitter tears. He knew he was doomed, of course, W. says. He knew he'd be executed. But he wept not because he knew he would die, but because he had been betrayed.

'*Without friends, no one would choose to live*', Danton said to himself, quoting from Aristotle. And when Robespierre added his signature to the warrant for Danton's arrest, Danton didn't even try to escape, W. says. He didn't try to leave France. He didn't call on his admirers to save him. His spirit was broken, this indomitable man. His strength had been tried, and found wanting. Friendship can only bear so much, W. says, and pauses. Betrayal!, cries W. Betrayal!

Is that how it will be, in the coming revolution?, W. wonders. Will I buy a sky-blue cloak and powder my wig? Will I sign W.'s death warrant? I have something of the *fanatic* about me, W. says. I'm ready to serve a greater cause. To give myself to something I barely understand.

Conference evening, on Greenwich lawns.

How many speakers we've heard! How many ideas! Sometimes, we have to admit, we were bored. Sometimes, we fell to drawing monkey butlers in our notebooks. Sometimes, W. wrote an obscenity in big letters in my notebook, or I drew something depraved in his. But at other times, we were exhilarated, set on fire by thought. We felt caught in the updraft of someone else's ideas. We felt flown like kites by the thoughts of others.

But now we're tired, after our day. Our limbs feel heavy; our eyes are closing.

W. has always believed that there are certain thoughts which come to you only in exhaustion, only once you've reached the end of your strength.

Hasn't he reached this point with his friends among the Essex postgraduates, time and time again? Haven't he and his housemates discovered the secrets of the universe after drunken nights at the bar?

The trouble is that what exhaustion reveals it also keeps to itself, W. says. What could he and his friends remember the next day of what they had discussed? What, of the truth that seemed to dawn between them? What, of *weary truth*, of the *truth of weariness*?

It's different with me, of course, for whom exhaustion

leads nowhere, W. says. What thoughts have ever come to him at the end of *our* nights of drinking? What has there ever been but formless horror and the kind of states only Edgar Allan Poe would know how to name?

We need to wake up, W. says. We need to revitalise ourselves. There's only one thing for it!

Sometimes, you need to be among the postgraduates, we agree. Sometimes you need to feel them alongside you, full of life, full of brilliance.

It's like swimming with dolphins, W. says. It's like snorkelling through a shoal of fish. You feel tiny electrical shocks on your skin. Your hair feels as though it's standing on end. Ah, what joy of brilliance they show! What *fleetness* of the mind!

Postgraduates are the *angels* of the academic world, we agree. They're between worlds — mediators between the heaven of full-time lecturers and the netherworld of the undergraduate. They teach — they often take seminars — but they are not a real part of the teaching staff. They study, it is true, but they're not entirely students, either.

They have a sense of what they want to achieve: an academic job, an academic career, but they know that there are very few such jobs, and very little chance of a career. They've fled from the world into academia, but they know they will most likely find themselves back where they came from, as though they'd dreamt up the entirety of their postgraduate lives.

Here we are among them, the angels, the Greenwich post-graduates. How *slim* they are! How *tall*, all dressed in black, and smoking their cigarettes! How *intense* they are, talking of their work, and weighing up the conference speakers! How *focused*, discussing ideas and only ideas...!

Postgraduates are the antennae of academia, W. says. They know everything about the latest thought from France, from Germany. About the latest *commentaries* on French and German thought by British and American academics. About the goings-on in British departments of philosophy, of *continental* philosophy. About possible job openings in this or that department, about possible postdoctoral research opportunities at this or that university.

There's no thought as *keen* as postgraduate thought, we agree. Nothing as effort-filled, as intense. Nothing in which the stakes are clearer. Because they're trying to escape, we agree. They're trying to be better than they are.

Some of them are careerists, it is true. Some of them are trying to claw their way into a job; they'll do anything to get there. Some of them are mediocrities-in-waiting, young fogeys with elbow patches on their jackets, ready to embody all the vices of full-time academic staff.

But other postgraduates are drawn to philosophy for the sake of philosophy, we agree. Others are drawn to thought for the sake of thought. They want to think against the world to which they will be forced to return. They want to think against *Britain*, this damnable country. They want a chance to protest in thought. They want to *redeem* their lives by thinking. To rise to a kind of secret glory, before it's time for them to leave the university, and return to the world.

There's no laughter like postgraduate laughter, W. says. There's nothing as dark. Nothing as knowing. It's death-row laughter, we agree. It's the laughter of those condemned to death.

Because they are condemned to death, the postgraduates around us. Shown the greatest of vistas, the whole landscape of Old Europe at their feet, and then thrown out into the world, they're condemned to a life without meaning, a life without succour, a life of shit in a world of shit...

They're martyrs, the British postgraduates, we agree. They're anchorites, like Saint Anthony in the desert. They're exiles from the world. They're *proletariats*, Marx would say. They're *individuals*, Kierkegaard would say. They waiting for the *revolution*, Marx would say. They're waiting for *grace*, Kierkegaard would say.

We are worn out by the postgraduates. They're too much for us! They're too brilliant! It's like looking in a terrible mirror. It's like seeing ourselves, robbed of self-satisfaction, robbed of our pandering. To think that we, too, were once postgraduates! To think that we, too, burned with the same black fire! And to think that by some strange miracle, by some lapse in the logic of the universe, we actually found jobs! To think that we — *we* — found ourselves in academic jobs!

My hotel room. W. takes his seat once again on the Chair of Judgement. It's time to list my short-comings! It's time to examine where I've gone wrong! To bury down to the root-cause!

'Would you call yourself a *moral* man?', W. asks. 'Would you call yourself a *man of honour*? Do other people *look up to you*? Are others *moved* by you, *inspired* by you?' A pause. And then: 'Do you think you've touched other people's lives — in a *good* way? Do you see yourself as a man of *thought*, a man of *profundity*, a man who will *leave a legacy*?'

These are the questions that constantly circle in W.'s head, as he knows they do not circle in mine, he says.

'How do you think you'll be judged?', W. asks. 'As a *serious* man? As a man attuned to *what matters most*?' And then, 'Will you be remembered as a *great soul*? As a *spiritual leader*?' A pause. And then: 'How do you understand your failure? Who do you measure yourself against? What standards have you failed to meet?'

Gin!, W. demands. He wants a respite from his judgement.

W. is soothed by the Plymouth Gin botanicals. He can taste the oris-root and the coriander seeds. He can taste the orange peel.

Plymouth Gin is our *realitätpunkt*, W. says. Our rallying

point, our place of safety. Sipping Plymouth Gin is always a homecoming, W. says. A return to what is most important.

If only we had some Vermouth, we could make Martinis, W. says. In the Plymouth Gin cocktail bar, they swill your glass with Vermouth, specially imported from America, and then pour it straight out. Only then do they fill the glass with Plymouth Gin and add a spiral of lemon peel, W. says. You need Vermouth only to pour it away, like an offering made to the gods, W. says.

More questions. 'How many people do you think you've offended?', W. asks. 'How many people have you irritated? Have you *angered*? How many people have tried to sue you?', because he knows that some have. 'How many people have tried to run you out of town?'

W. begins again. 'How many appetites have you spoilt? How many people have you put off their dinner? What would you say is your most *irritating* trait? Your most *rage-inducing* one?' And then, 'What do you think your clothes say about you? And your hair? Your shoes? Does the way you dress befit your role as a would-be thinker? As a would-be *philosopher*?'

Still more questions. 'Do you think you have a *noble* face? A *dignified* bearing? Do you think you have the *physiognomy* of a thinker? An *intelligent* face? Do your *rolls of fat* make you uncomfortable? Do you think obesity gives you *gravitas*? *Presence*?' He pauses. 'At what stage would you consider *gastric bypass surgery*? Have you ever thought of *liposuction*? Do you think you come across as a *happy* fat man, or as a *sad* fat man? At what stage will you have your mouth sewn up?

'Of what are you most guilty?', W. asks. 'What is your

greatest source of shame? What is your greatest failing? *Do* you think you've failed? *Do* you think you should be ashamed? *Do* you have any real sense of guilt?' And then, 'What do you think you *add* to the world?', W. asks. 'What do you think you *subtract*? What is your *net worth* to existence? Do you think you've added to the balance of *goodness* in the cosmos, or of *evil*? Are you on the side of the angels or the devils?'

'How do you think you can make amends?', W. asks. '*Do* you think you can make amends? How do you think you can make reparations for damages to intellectual reputation? For emotional damage? For *digestive* damage?

'Where do you think you stand in the *great chain of thinkers*?', W. asks. 'With what *historical* figure do you most identify? What *philosophical* figure? How would you rank yourself in a list of contemporary philosophers?' And then, 'Do you think you've *understood your time*? *Brought it to expression* in some way? Are you a *diagnoser* of your times, or a *symptom* of your times? Are you a cultural *physician*, or a cultural *patient*?'

W.'s exhausted, he says. The judgement is nearly over. A final round!

'Do you think you *fool* people?', W. asks. 'Can others read your stupidity in your eyes, do you think? Can they see your idiocy in your gait? Your posture?' And then, 'Do you have a sense of your idiocy — a real sense? Do you grasp just how desperately you've fallen short?'

Dawn. Daylight behind the blinds. The judgement's over. W. reads out a passage from Kierkegaard, which he copied into his notebook:

What does God want? He wants souls able to praise,
adore, worship, and thank him — the business of an-
gels. And what pleases him even more than the praise
of angels is a human being who, in the last lap of this
life, when God seemingly changes into sheer cruelty,
nevertheless continues to believe that God is love, that
God does it out of love.

If he's cruel to me, it's out of love, W. says. It is meant as
the highest kindness, when he sits on the Chair of Judgement
exploring the many compromises of my life, my betrayals and
half-measures. Who else would have taken notice? Who else
would have tried to teach me *the meaning of sin*?

Ah, would that he had a similar tutor! Would that someone had the same interest in him! But perhaps my ingratitude
is, for W., only a version of God's cruelty. Perhaps my *moan-*
ing in protest, as he sits above me on the Chair of Judgement,
is only a way for God to test the extremity of W.'s love.

Morning. The Royal Observatory, high on the hill. This is where the first *international terrorist incident* took place, W. says, reading from a plaque. A young French anarchist attempted to blow up the Observatory, to blow up Greenwich Mean Time...

To change time, to change the order of time: isn't that the aim of any revolution?, W. says. We have to recover the dimension of *possibility*. The dimension of the *infinite!*

Time touched by eternity: he's always found this. Kierkegaard phrase very moving, W. says. There is the *time that passes*, Kierkegaard argues — this instant, then that, which we merely endure, which merely carry us along. And then there is *time touched by eternity*, Kierkegaard says, which allows past, present and future to assume their true role in our lives, as *phases of development*. Once time has been touched by eternity, we no longer simply persist in time, but deepen and grow. We come to *exist temporally*, living towards a future that we earn by our deepening, by our growth: that's what Kierkegaard argues.

Time touched by eternity: is that what is meant by *revolutionary time*?, W. wonders. Is that why the French revolutionaries renamed the days of the week? Is that why they remade the calendar?

Tarrday, that's we should rename Monday, W. says.

Krasznahorkaiday: it's a bit of a mouthful, but that's what Tuesday should become. And *Weilday* instead of Wednesday. *Cohenday* instead of Thursday. Friday can be *Deleuzeday*. And *Rosenzweigday*, for the day of the Jewish Sabbath. And Sunday: *Kierkegaard-day*: why not?, W. says.

The view from the hill. The City, across the river, all bombast, with its great towers to Mammon. The domes of Greenwich Naval College. The low-rise estates on this side of the river, to which the poor of London moved when their houses were bulldozed.

Sometimes, W. longs for a great explosion in the sky. For a nearby star to burst across the heavens. For a comet's head, blazing towards us. Ah, why is it easier to imagine the end of the world than to imagine the end of capitalism?

Tottenham, emerging from the Underground.

W.'s not surprised that a madman came to sit next to us on the train. Did the madman sense that we had something in common? Did he believe us to be *akin*, somehow? Like-minded, somehow?

He looked like one of Tarkovsky's holy fools, lost in the mud, W. says. He looked like Alexander Kaidanovsky in *Stalker*. A man of great sadness, but of great hope, too. Of course, our madman was a *religious* man, as all madmen are religious, W. says. He was an *apocalyptic* man, as all mad-men are apocalyptic.

The madman spoke of the end of the world. W. nodded in agreement. He spoke of the last judgement. W. affirmed what he said. He spoke of the remnant, of the last stand of the righteous. Yes!, W. exclaimed, a number of times. He spoke of Nostradamus, and W. demurred. He spoke of astrology, of the lining up of the fixed signs of Aquarius, Leo, Taurus and Scorpio in the shape of a cross, and W. kept quiet. But when the madman quoted chunks of the Book of Revelations, W. brightened again.

'*And there fell a great star from heaven, burning as if it were a lamp*', the madman said, as he rose and set off down the carriage. '*And it fell upon the third part of the rivers, and upon the fountains of waters...*', he cried back as he wandered down the carriage. '*And the name of the star is called Worm-wood!*', he shouted, turning and facing us for the last time.

We mustn't be afraid to see our world in apocalyptic terms, W. says. In *religious* terms. The language of the Last Days is wholly appropriate to our times.

We know what is coming. We know that a new dawn — the opposite of dawn — will spread its dark rays from the horizon. We know that the time will come to put down our pens and close our books...

Climatic catastrophe. Financial catastrophe. W. quotes the prophet Joel: '*the rivers of waters are dried up, and the fire hath devoured the pastures of the wilderness*'. And he remembers what the prophet Jeremiah saw in the ruins of Jerusalem: the earth without form and void. The heavens without light. The very mountains reeling...

He had a strange dream the other night, W. says. I had become a kind of *priest*. A *Hindu* priest, with lines of ash on my forehead, and my hair long and pulled back into a topknot.

I was speaking the Law, W. says. Not about the Law, but the Law itself, as if it could be spoken. As if I would know the Law.

I spoke in a low murmur, W. says, that was inseparable from a rumbling all around us. The skies were darkening, W. says. Storm-clouds were massing in the sky.

It was like the Biblical disasters, W. says. The great flood. The plague of locusts. The destruction of Sodom. But it was worse, W. says. It was more terrible, even as it seemed to leave everything intact.

The destruction of the world *was* the world: that's what

suddenly became clear to him, in his dream, W. says. The end of the world was already present in every *detail* of the world. The *eschaton* was *already* here; the apocalypse was *already* happening.

Middlesex University has the crappiest of campuses, we agree. It looks like a primary school from the '70s, all terrapins, all plastic chairs. But from the crappiest campus, the greatest thought. . .

So what are *we* doing here?, W. wonders. Why did they invite *us*? You'd have thought they'd have wanted us to *keep away*. That we'd have been *banned*, not invited.

There are people at Middlesex who can *think*, for God's sake! And now *we're* here, we who are in no way capable of thought. We'll have to depend on our charm (on W.'s charm). We'll have to use our natural wit (W.'s natural wit). — 'And you can do your monkey dance for them', W. says. 'That should buy us some time before they lynch us'.

Morning beer before our paper. Dutch courage at the first open pub we find.

Ah, why did he bring me with him for his Middlesex debut?, W. wonders. What will his Middlesex friends make of me? 'What is *he* doing here?': that's the question W. will see in their suddenly narrowed eyes. You, we understand, but *him*. . . ?

I confuse his thinking friends, W. says. Of course, they know at once I'm not a fellow thinker, a fellow thought-adventurer. For a moment — and for no more than that, since such thinkers have other things to reflect upon — they wonder whether I am not to W. as W. is to them — a kind of slow-witted brother, a cousin and fellow, one who needs encouragement, *bringing on...*

That's why they smile at me, despite everything, W. says. It's why they make some semblance of including me in their conversations, turning to me as though I could understand what they were saying, as though I were capable of following their accounts of their struggles with thought.

It's why they speak to me of the *shrivelling* of thought, when thought contracts like a pair of testicles in the cold, W. says. It's why they speak to me of thought's *bolting*, when thought branches wildly, uncontrollably, far beyond anything you could control. It's why they speak to me of *cancers* of thought, when thought is hollowed out from within, by doubts and unconfidence; and of *locusts* of thought, when thought is devoured from without, by illness and misfortune, poverty and abuse.

It's why they speak to me of the fear of *madness*, of opening their minds too wide. That's the thing they all fear, W. says. That's the terror of the real thinker.

W.'s Middlesex friends are on the margins of the philosophy department, he says. They're research fellows, kept on contracts, never knowing whether they'll be renewed, never knowing whether they'll have a job next year.

They speak with irony of the misery of their working conditions. Of precarity and underemployment. Of the loneliness of the long distance postdoctoral researcher.

But they still smile, W. says. They have their studies, after all. They have their thought-paths. They know their *brilliance*, W. says. They feel it throbbing in their temples.

What *conversations* he's had with his Middlesex friends!, W. says. What late-night dialogues! They're so young! They're full of burning thoughts! Blazing thoughts! Philosophy is on fire inside them!

W.'s Middlesex friends remind him of the young in Robert Bresson's films, full of life, full of beauty, but hopelessly lost in the devil's playground that is the world. They remind him of the young *suicides* of Bresson's films, driven to death because there is nothing for them in life, choosing to die by their own hand rather than live hypocritically.

They die of the *truth*, Bresson's young people, W. says. They die because of what they see in themselves of the world. They die because of their sense of the *corruption* of their innocence, because they are angels and because they are tarnished, W. says.

Haven't the Middlesex researchers confessed to W. of their terrible melancholias, of *disorders of the spirit* that their effort to think has only driven deeper? Hasn't he had to pull them back from the brink?

We must be tireless in our support of real thinkers, W. says. We must never close our eyes. The real thinker is close to death, close to suicide. The real thinker is subject to impersonal agonies, to interstellar tortures. They real thinker has set out alone to the heart of thought's continent, all the way to the pole. And some have even returned from that pole, their hair streaked with frost, their tears frozen on their cheeks. They've seen the broken ice of the Arctic of thought and the crevassed plains of the *Antarctic* of thought.

Thoughts should shatter the frozen sea within us, that's what Kafka wrote, W. says. And that's what he's seen in the eyes of his Middlesex friends: a shattering. The fact that a shattering has occurred with tremendous force. That the landscape of thought has been broken and reassembled. That it has heaved upwards in a kind of earthquake, and crashed back down again, changed in its every detail in a way only a true thinker could understand.

What do you think his Middlesex friends see when they see us, with our permanent jobs?, W. asks. What, when we stand before them, with our lectureships and our indolence? *Compromise*: that's what they see. *Bourgeois philosophy!...*

The Middlesex researchers will find us wanting, we who have grown fat in our university jobs, W. says. They'll see that our ideas are only middle class ideas, and that our despair is only a remembered despair, a *sham* despair.

Middlesex campus. How many times have we wandered through a university in which we're about to give a presentation, dread mounting inside us like bile? How many times have we walked like men condemned, vowing that this time it will be different; that this time it will all come right?

Coffee! We need coffee! Coffee will make us able to think more keenly; one espresso, another, and it will all become clear. A third cup, and we'll swell with self-belief. A fourth, and we'll be certain that our thought is of world-historical significance. Epochal significance!

But they only serve instant coffee on campus, and no revelation comes no matter how many cups we drink.

We were altogether too *pathetic* for our Middlesex audience, W. says, on the train back to the city. Our vague communism. Our *messianic pathos*: what need had they for that?

My beard didn't fool them, W. says. Nor did his half-beard. They were looking for something else. Something tougher. They didn't want to hear about exilic themes in the work of Marx. They were uninterested from the first in *Marx's messianism*.

W. opened his notebook, and read aloud:

> *The present generation is like the Jews whom Moses*
> *led through the wilderness. It has not only a new world*
> *to conquer, it must go under in order to make room for*
> *men who are able to cope with a new world.*

'That's Marx', he told our listeners. And then, 'The reference is to the book of *Exodus*, of course'. Hostility from our audience. They were unimpressed. This is no time for religion!, said their folded arms. Less pathos, more precision!, said their pursed lips. The banks are collapsing, and this is what you have to tell us?, said their filed-sharp teeth.

Moses and his people left Egypt, where they were slaves,

and, in obedience to God's call, headed into the desert in search of the promised land, W. said. The desert: who would go there?, he continued. The 'great and terrible wilderness', the Bible calls it, with no grass for pasture, where thirst and starvation would drive you mad. A wasteland, a damned place, the refuge of the devil: who would heed Moses' call for exodus?, W. asked.

But heed it they did, hundreds of thousands of them, pursued by the chariots of the Pharaoh, W. said. Go they did, with God amongst them, for wasn't God, too, a pilgrim with the children of Israel?

Then I took the baton. For forty years they wandered, I said. It was forty years before they reached Canaan. Why so long?, I asked rhetorically. Because they had to rid themselves of the memory of captivity, the memory of Egypt, I answered. Because a generation had to be born and raised who knew nothing of slavery.

Then W. again. The young: everything, for Moses, depended on them, he said. The young were the fruit of the years of tribulation. It was the same for Marx, for whom the proletariat was always young, fiercely young. But until then?, W. asked rhetorically. Until the proletariat came who had no memory of their slavery and of the land of their captivity? Wandering, W. said. Endless wandering.

The Talmud tells us that it is forbidden to grow old, W. said. He was thinking of our young audience at this point, he says. Of the Middlesex researchers, sitting around us in a semicircle, with a dagger in their hearts, and ice on their lips. W. was dreaming of those to come after us, after our *going under*, he says.

We're not young enough!, W. says, as we step from the

train. Not ardent enough! We are what must be overcome. We need to be purged, we agree. Put up against the wall as counter-revolutionaries. And only then, without us, might liberation unfold. Only then might the world begin to overcome its bondage.

Breakfast. Muffins and orange pekoe tea. A fitting repast before revisiting his alma mater, W. says. He's returning to the spawning ground of his academic life, like a salmon leaping upriver.

How many years has it been?, W. wonders. How long, since he left the University of Essex? How long, since they all left, he and the other former Essex postgraduates? Ah, what would they think of him now, his erstwhile comrades?

Those were political times, W. says. The late '70s, the early '80s... Memories of the revolts of May 1968 were still alive. Memories of *British Sounds*, the film Jean-Luc Godard made on Essex University campus.

W. describes the last scene: a bloodied hand rising from the mud. — 'Godard cut his own hand for that. He wouldn't use fake blood'.

We should cut our own hands, W. says. Our own throats! Then people might believe us. Then they might believe that we have something to say.

He had a very strange dream the other night, W. says. The two of us were on trial for something serious — what, he didn't know. The courtroom was deserted, W. says. There was no judge there to bang the gavel. No defence team, no prosecution. No policemen. But we were guilty, we knew we were. We'd found ourselves guilty...

'Has our time come?', W. asked me. Ages ago, I told him. — 'Then what's keeping them?', he asked. The judgement came too late, I told him. There are no hangmen, there is no firing squad. The army have all deserted their posts. The very institutions of the law are empty, their doors swinging open, files blowing about in the wind.

'Then who will carry through the sentence?', W. asked. There's no one to carry through the sentence, I told him. — 'Who will lead us to the gallows?' There's no one to lead us to the gallows. — 'Are we to strangle ourselves?' I'll strangle you, and you strangle me, and we'll see where that gets us, I told him.

The real philosopher has philosophical dreams, W. says. Leibniz dreamed of monads, and Spinoza of infinite substance. Heidegger dreamed of the Being of beings, and Levinas of the face of the Other.

He only dreams of me, W. says. What does that mean?

Interrogative schoolgirls on a Colchester bus. — 'Where are you going?' 'Why do you dress like that?' Yes, where are we going? Why *do* we dress like this? The nine-year-olds are panicking us. — 'Didn't anyone tell you not to talk to strangers?'

Essex University. Straight to the Student Union. — 'We'll be in the bar', we've told everyone we know. Constancy is always admired, we agree. People should know where to find you.

We order beers, then whiskey, then beers, then whiskey, then chips, then beers, then whiskey, then another beer and another whiskey, then chips. A balanced diet, W. says. All the major food groups.

Essex Student Union bar. This is where he used to drink as a postgraduate, W. says. It's where he learned to drink, he who had been near-teetotal before — and to smoke, he who had never smoked a cigarette in his life.

Do I have any sense of what it was like to feel part of a *generation*?, W. says. Can I understand what it was to have something expected of you, to have faith placed in you? A sense that something was happening — something that could only have happened *there* and *then*?

Did they think they could change the world?, I ask him.

Not the world, but thought, W. says. They believed that they could change thinking, that they were the beginning of something, a new movement, that they augured what Britain might become: a *thinking country*, just as France is a *thinking country*, just as Germany was a *thinking country*.

This is where they spoke, W. says, and of great things. This is where they *spoke* — can I understand what that means? To speak, to be swept along by great currents. To be borne along, part of something, some ongoing debate. And for that debate to have stakes, to *matter*. For thought to become *personal*, to concern the most intimate details of your life. Ah, how can he convey it to me, who has never known intellectual life, intellectual friendship, who barely knows what friendship means, let alone the intellect?

A life of the mind, that's what they'd chosen. A life of the mind for postgraduates from all over Britain, a kind of *internal exile*. Because that's what it means to be a thinker in Britain: a kind of internal exile. They'd turned their backs on their families, on old friends. On the places of their birth. They'd turned from their old lives, their old jobs, old lovers. They'd travelled from the four corners of the country to be remade here, to be reborn. Essex, Essex: what joy it was in that dawn to be alive...

This is where they *spoke*, says W. very insistently. Do I know what it means to speak? This is where they argued. Do I know what it means to argue? This is where they fought in thought. And this is where they *loved*, too, says W. The Student Union Bar: this is where thought was alive, where thought was life, where thought was a matter of life and death...

This is where they *spoke,* W. says. Where voices trembled. Where voices rose. They laughed, and the laughter died away. Did they weep? No doubt there was weeping. No doubt some wept. This is where they promised themselves to thought. This is where they *signed the covenant...*

It was like serving together in a secret army, W. says. Even now, when he meets them, the former postgraduates of Essex, he sees the sign. Even now, it's clear; they are marked — they were marked then. Thought was life. Thought was their lives. They were remade in thought's crucible. They flared up renewed from thought's fire.

They learned to read French thought in French, German thought in German. They studied Latin and ancient Greek. Imagine it: a British person reading ancient Greek! They crossed the channel and studied in Paris. They plunged into Europe and studied in Rome. They visited the great archives. They read in the great libraries.

They were *becoming European,* W. says. Do I have any idea what that meant: to *become European*? Some of them even learned to *speak* other languages. Imagine it: a British person speaking French. Imagine it: a Briton in Berlin, conversing in German...

They went en masse to a two-week conference in Italy. Imagine it: British postgraduates en masse at a two-week conference in Italy. They played chess in the sun, and drank wine until their teeth turned red. Italy! The Mediterranean! Who among them had ever been to Italy, or the Mediterranean? Who had any idea of Italy, or the Mediterranean?

The sun burned them brown, imagine! Their pallid British

bodies, brown. Their teeth, red. The sun turned them mad. They thought as Van Gogh painted: without a hat, and in the full sun. Hatless, in the full sun, they became madmen and madwomen of thought.

Essex broke them. Essex rebuilt them. Essex broke their Britishness, their provincialness. Essex gave them philosophy. It gave them politics. It gave them friendship, and by way of philosophy, by way of politics. They were close to Europe, terribly close. Like Hölderlin's Greece, Europe was the *fire from heaven* for the Essex postgraduate. Like Hölderlin's Germany, Britain, staid and dull, was to be set on fire by heaven.

Ah, what happened to them all, the postgraduates of Essex?, W. muses. What happened to the last generation — the last generation of Essex postgraduates?

Some escaped. Some went elsewhere. But others fell back into Britishness — fell into the drowning pool of Britishness. They drowned, gasping for air, finding no air, in Britain.

Hadn't they seen too much? Hadn't they learnt what they lacked? Hadn't they a sense now of great thought, of great politics? Hadn't their skies been full of light, full of the heavenly fire?

Essex University. God, what a terrible campus! The towers are like the towers of Mordor, we agree. Like the Crags of Doom. In the tiny bathroom on our floor, a neon light flashes on and off. I bring W. to show him. It's like something from David Lynch, we agree. It feels like a symbol, but of what? There'll be a murder here, later, we agree. Or a suicide. One or other of us will throw ourselves from the tower, from one of the crags of doom. Or perhaps we'll both hurl ourselves down to the concrete...

To Wivehoe!, W. cries, with a sudden show of longing...

The Essex postgraduates all lived in Wivenhoe, a fishing village not far from the campus, W. says. There, they would stroll singly or in pairs along the river. *I'm taking the river air*, one postgraduate would say to another, as they passed. *We're taking the ozone*, one pair of postgraduate strollers would say to another.

The thinker needs a milieu, W. says. A *place* to think. Kant in his Konigsberg, walking the same route every day. Kierkegaard in his Copenhagen, wandering among the crowds...

The thinker needs regularity! External structure! The thinker needs discipline, if he's in it for the long haul, W. says.

Structure and discipline: isn't that what I lack?, W. says. I am a *chaotic* man, he says. A man without pattern.

Didn't I lurch my way through my philosophical studies (my so-called studies)?, W. says. Didn't I *twitch* through my Sanskrit studies and *flop* through my musical studies? Didn't I *jerk* as I tried to learn ancient Greek, and *spasm* as I tried to read Augustine in the original?

Of course, you can't study on your own, that was my mistake, W. says. You need to be part of something, part of a larger whole. You have to be able to believe in yourself as a scholar, W. says. As a would-be *philosopher!* And you have to be able to believe that the world might be *changed* as a result of your thinking. That it will all lead somewhere!

They believed in themselves, W. says: that's what marked them out, he and his fellow Essex postgraduates. *They* believed in the importance of what they were studying. *They* believed in their own youth, their own promise. Why, they could be new Spinozas, new Scotuses! Oh, they knew that no one would read them, W. says. They knew that there was no chance of finding an academic job, of getting a lectureship. They knew that their legacy would never be passed down to the next generation. Theirs was a *last stand*: it was quite obvious to the Essex postgraduates. Theirs was the last chance of thought.

W. set himself a particularly rigorous schedule of study when he lived in Wivenhoe, he says. Four hours at his desk, and then a walk to take the ozone... A light lunch, followed by practice at his classical guitar... An hour at his German, or an hour at his Greek. An hour at his *Hebrew*... Then four more hours at his desk before dinner. And after dinner, a walk along the river, W. says. A walk to take the ozone, and to let his studies of the day knit themselves together in his head...

There were dozens of Essex postgraduates living in Wivenhoe. Dozens, for whom philosophy was *life itself*, for whom Wivenhoe might as well have been ancient Athens or Enlightenment Jena. They lived in poverty, of course, W. says. They lived on welfare. They barely ate. They drank, of course. They drank a great deal!

The British person *has* to drink in order to do philosophy, W. says. To drink away their Britishness! Their uptightness! Their reservedness! Their aversion to discussion! To looking one another in the eye!

Centuries of positivism have left their scars on Britain, W. says. Centuries of the hatred of metaphysics, of religion! The British have the *worst possible attitude* to intellectual speculation, W. says. They are the most *provincial* of people. The most *inward-looking* of people. The most *suburban*!

Really, British thought is a contradiction in terms, W. says. British ideas! The British intellectual is an oxymoron, he says, because the British despise intellectuals. Because British intellectuals despise themselves.

How they drank, the Essex postgraduates!, W. says. They needed to drink! They had to drink! Drinking was a discipline, for the Essex postgraduate. And smoking! How they smoked!, W. says. The British would-be thinker has to smoke, W. says. To strike against their health and vitality. Against rosy cheeks! Against bright eyes!

Only ill-health can shatter British complacency, W. says.

Only late nights and despair! The Essex postgraduates knew they had to declare war on themselves, if they were to think. They knew they had to destroy the reign of Britain in their souls, W. says.

The bus hurtles through the countryside, branches crashing against the windows. A bus full of academics! A bus full of enemies! — 'Oh God!', W. wails.

Academic philosophers hate real philosophers, W. says. Just as scholars of music hate real musicians. Just as scholars of literature hate poets and novelists. They hate us!, W. says, of our fellow passengers. They hate *him*!

Oh, they don't hate us personally, W. says. They don't even know us. They're completely indifferent to us! That's part of the problem. — 'Do you think anyone on this bus knows our names? Of course not!' But they *would* hate us, if they knew us. They would lynch us immediately, if they understood anything about us.

We should be going to Wivenhoe, W. says. But the conference bus is heading in the opposite direction. Ah, why did we get on board? Why do we always do what's wrong for us?

The conference dinner. Alain Badiou, sitting all alone.

Why don't we ask to join him? Why don't we introduce ourselves, and sit down beside him? W. could speak in his soft French, and I could fetch a bottle of wine and some glasses.

We could lament the fatuity of what passes itself off as ethics in both public discourse and the university, and analyse the supplanting of real philosophy by so-called *applied* ethics (badminton ethics). We could mull over the origin of the great French philosophy of the '60s, and the decline of German Critical Theory since the '60s.

We could agree, too, that the world-historical mission of philosophy is far from over, far from gone. We could agree that there is to be no more 'continental' woolliness, no more Derridean equivocation: that the time has come to think clearly, decisively!

We could reflect on the destiny of the notion of the infinite in both philosophical thought and mathematical thought. We could muse upon *Koch Curves* and the *Kimberling shuffle*, upon *non-averaging sets* and *non-dividing sets*, and consider the nature of love, of art, of politics, of science, as *forms of truth*.

And perhaps Badiou could entertain us with anecdotes of his own life as a thinker, and perhaps we could entertain him with some anecdotes of our own...

But why should Alain Badiou want to speak to us? He's a man of rigour and mathematical precision! He's a man of politics, of real political commitment!

On Saturday morning, when W. is eating crumpets with Sal, and I'm still lying in bed, Badiou has already jotted down a few notes for *Being and Event III*; he's already drafted an obituary essay for a dead fellow thinker — a thought-enemy, granted, but a worthy adversary. He's already spoken to Sylvain Lazarus on the phone, about their campaign for the *sans-papiers* ...

Badiou has already had several thoughts concerning his defence of Maoism, and looked over the English translation of one of his plays. He's already skim-read articles from a dozen international newspapers, and caught up with his emails, replying to Žižek, writing to Jacques Rancière. He's already written a brief blurb for a forthcoming book by Jean-Luc Nancy (much better than *my* blurb for Jean-Luc Nancy, W. says). He's already jotted down the points he wants to cover in his open letter on behalf of the poor of the Paris Banlieus, which he means to send to *Le Monde*.

Badiou has already had his coffee and croissant, and a freshly squeezed orange juice, and sat out on his terrace in his shirtsleeves, taking in the morning sun, turning over his latest ideas in his head. How many thoughts has he had since he got up? Countless thoughts! How many notions, waiting to coalesce? Countless notions!

How much outrage does Badiou feel, really feel, at the triumph of the right in France? Great outrage! How much horror does he feel at the dreadful plight of the poor? Enormous horror! But Badiou *acts* on his outrage and his horror. He writes polemical articles to publish in mainstream papers. He circulates petitions and strides out onto the streets.

Ah, how many demonstrations has Badiou seen? How many street-battles? How many cobblestones has he torn up from the ground to throw at police? How many truncheons have bounced off his head? He can remember Althusser as a contemporary, Balibar as a whippersnapper. He remembers the Maoist Barthes, the Maoist Kristeva just home from China ... And he remembers the *Restoration* of the '80s, when every leftist dream was lost.

But what would Alain Badiou make of us? What would he conclude? Enemies, he would think. No, not even that, Badiou would think. — '*Pas enemies. Les tosseurs*'. But perhaps he wouldn't think anything at all. Perhaps he'd just look through us, as if, like evil for Plato, we didn't really exist.

For the mathematical philosopher, vagueness doesn't exist, not really; it's only a deficiency of precision. And for the political philosopher, pathos doesn't exist, except in the glint of starlight, impersonal and remote, on the eyeglasses of the militant, hurling bricks at the police.

The loos aren't working, I tell W. on the train out of London. They're blocked up with toilet roll. — 'Go and unblock them!,' W. says. 'Do your bit for redemption!'

W. recalls what happened on the bus to Memphis, on our doomed Dogma lecture tour of America. We'd headed to the back seats, by the toilet. You get less travel-sick there, that was my reasoning. And you can watch everyone, you can see what's going on. W. was happy to be led.

But something terrible must have happened in the toilet, we realised slowly. The smell! My God! W. berated himself. Why does he always follow me into *the teeth of the catastrophe?*

A passenger gasped and crossed herself when she opened the toilet door. — 'Don't do it!', we told her. But she came back a moment later with a portable air freshener, holding it out before her as she opened the door, and spraying it in the sign of the cross.

Minutes passed. We heard humming from inside. And then she emerged, smiling. She's cleaned the loo, said W. She's cleaned it, for us. For everyone! We sat in awe. That's sainthood, said W.

It is *small kindnesses* that redeem history, W. says. Small kindnesses — that's all we have left as the great machines grind on all about us. The great political machines, the great economic machines. The great machines of regeneration ...

Small kindnesses, W. says. The miracle of goodness, which appears only in isolated acts, in stupid, senseless generosity, in the kind of gratuitous altruism that you find in Russian novels, in the *holy idiots* of Dostoevsky and Grossman ...

He wishes I were a holy idiot, W. says, and not just an idiot. He wishes I would show a Dostoevskian innocence or a Grossmanian selflessness. He wishes I were an *un*worldly man, instead of being all too worldly, *super*-worldly, W. says.

W. sees me in his mind's eye wandering barefoot and almost naked in the severest frosts, driving away all self-love and pride, and seeking to evoke nothing but contempt in my fellow human beings, all the while cultivating love for my enemies and persecutors. He sees me voluntarily taking on humiliation and insults to achieve the proper depth of meekness and goodness of heart. He imagines me as a *fool for Christ*, living in patience and unceasing prayer...

And when he comes to? There I am, before him again, a fool for no one, an idiot for no cause. There I am, having rejected all dignity, all self-love and pride, having accepted humiliation and insults, and evoking nothing but contempt in my fellow human beings because *I cannot do otherwise*...

There was only one moment in W.'s life when he showed great compassion, he says.

It was snowing, he remembers. No one was on the campus. No one except W., who had gone there to prepare his defence against his redundancy. Who else would have come into work on such a day?

He met her by chance, he says, as he rounded a corner. She stumbled into him, having slipped on the ice — he caught her, stood her up, and recognised her as the manager who had put his name forward to be sacked.

As she faced him, he saw tears in her eyes. She was crying — why? She opened her mouth to speak. She paused. And then she said, 'It was nothing personal'.

It was nothing personal. But of course it was something personal! She'd singled him out from all his colleagues. Sack W.!, she'd told the redundancy committee.

Tears brimming in her eyes... The frosty air... The deserted campus... Ice everywhere, as in bleakest Siberia... And what did he do, W., to his oppressor? What, to one who deserved no quarter? He embraced her, he says. He put his arms around her, like one of Dostoevsky's idiots.

He was brought up to be compassionate, W. says. He was brought up to show mercy and forgiveness. And so he embraced her, there in the snow. — 'Everything's going to be okay...'

Oxford. The dreaming spires. We're in *enemy territory*, we agree. We've been parachuted deep behind enemy lines. It's a suicide mission. A soiling-ourselves mission. — 'Go on, you start'.

Oxford! Why do we come here? Why, year after year? W. feels as though he's suffocating, he says. As though he can't breathe and his hands are clawing the air. Being buried alive is bad enough, W. says, but being buried alive with an idiot! At least I should amuse him. At least I should do something funny. But Oxford is too much even for me. It's like going around with a sulky ape.

Why does Oxford always make him think of Poland?, W. wonders. It's dialectics, he says. It's because Poland is the *opposite* of Oxford. Because Poland is a place of thought, a place where thought is valued, and Oxford is a place *without* thought, a place where thought is despised.

Poland: that's where it all began, so many years ago, we agree. Our collaboration, our dog and pony show.

Is there such a thing as *friendship at first sight?*, W. wonders. Well, that's what happened in Poland, in Wrocław, when he saw my *Adam Ant dancing*: friendship at first sight.

Ah, he still remembers it, W. says: in the middle of the

meal held in honour of the British delegation in Wrocław, I pushed back my chair to demonstrate *Adam Ant dancing*. He remembers when I took to the dancefloor, recreating *Adam Ant dancing* from the *Prince Charming* video. And he remembers how the Polish postgraduates followed me; how they, too, pushed back their chairs and took to the dancefloor, likewise recreating *Adam Ant dancing* from the *Prince Charming* video.

'*Here is a man who does not know shame*', W. thought to himself. '*Not only this, he seems to encourage others to forget their shame*'. And soon W., too, pushed back his chair and took to *Adam Ant dancing*.

And our Polish hosts, who were so generous in organising a meal in our honour, sat by, smiling and drumming their fingers, perhaps wondering if there wasn't a British tradition — a British *philosophical* tradition — of *Adam Ant dancing* at the beginning of a conference.

And when we sat down, breathless, faces flushed? When we pulled our chairs back to the table, ready for our sauerkraut and dumplings at the dinner held in our honour? W. felt a new kind of *lightness*, he said. A new *dizziness*. For what had he known, hitherto, of *pure joy*? What had he known of the sense of *abandonment* that marks pure joy?

Henceforward, I blazed a trail ahead of him that he knew he'd have to follow. Henceforth, it was joy that sprang ahead of us — ahead of *me*, and drawing me on, and now ahead of *him*, too, and drawing *him* on — a kind of joy attached to nothing in particular.

It's happening just as I predicted, W. says. The collapse of the universities. The collapse of civilisation. Don't you realise how *good* we're having it?, I've always said to him. These are the *best of times*, I've said, over and again. You think *this* is bad? It's going to get *worse, much worse*, I've told him, and I was right. Some idiots are savants, W. reflects. Like that guy in *Rain Man*.

The corpse of the university floats face down in the water, that's what I always tell him, W. says. We're poking it with sticks. None of us can believe it. Is it really dead, the university?, W. asks me. Is that really its bloated, blue-faced corpse? Yes, it really is dead, and there it is, floating, face down, I tell him. There's no point pretending otherwise, not anymore. The university is dead, and there is its corpse.

Oh, there are *signs* of life in the university, I tell W. It *seems* that it's alive. But that life is the life of maggots, I tell W., devouring the substance of the university from the inside, living on its rotting.

The corpse of the university is a breeding ground, I tell W. The corpse is where Capital comes to lay its eggs. The university is that rotten place where Capital deposits its eggs...

Christchurch Meadows. This is the *walk of death*, we agree. You think you're escaping Oxford, as you head out along the river, but really you're only going more deeply into Oxford. It's a city even the Situationist couldn't redeem, W. says. You think you're leaving it behind, all the nonsense, all the stuffiness, the whole stage-set let's-pretend antiquarianism, W. says, but really you're only *confirming* it. How many poor idiots like us have thought they could escape Oxford while in Oxford, W. says, only to find themselves more deeply immersed in Oxford than ever?

It's part of the *Oxford rhythm*, the Christchurch Meadows walk, we agree. The way it grants you the *illusion of freedom*, only to draw you in more deeply. The way it seems to open the door, and make Oxford less like a prison. Imagine how many poor idiots like us have marched up the Cherwell, W. says. Up the fucking Cherwell, congratulating themselves on having escaped!

Meanwhile, Oxford is laughing at you. The Oxonians are laughing at you. The spires of the Oxford colleges are laughing at you, and you might as well kill yourself. In the end, we are the *dupes* of Oxford, we agree. We've been duped by it, thoroughly duped. We're Oxford's idiots. We came here because our confreres came here, because our *annual conference* is held here, because our society likes to borrow the prestige of Oxford, hiring out a college to let us play-pretend at being Oxonians.

We laugh at our confrères but we are as trapped as they are: walking through the meadows as they do, walking out along the river as they do, walking out of Oxford for a bit of fresh air as they do, really we're only ever breathing in the *foul air of Oxford* as they do, W. says. We're like all the other parasites in the *rotting flesh* of Oxford, W. says. Walking out in order to come back in, walking away in order to return: that's the dreadful rhythm of Oxford, we agree.

But in the end, Oxford's time will come. It is coming. Of course it is! The rough beast is slouching towards Oxford, too. For a time it will be permitted to continue, this façade of old England, this façade of study, this façade of research. But it is coming, the privatisation of thought, and not even Oxford will resist it.

'After tragedy, farce', W. says, remembering Marx. And after farce? This. Us. Christchurch Meadows.

Who are we amusing? Who laughs at our slapstick? — 'Something in us doesn't know that we've died', W. says. 'Something in us doesn't grasp our destruction'.

Who's going to finish us off? Why haven't they done it already? For whom are we the insects that race around when a rock is lifted? Someone needs amusing, so they're letting us live, W. says. Some idiot god, with drool running down his chin.

Our failure; again and again our failure. Why don't we learn? Why do we never learn from our mistakes? But if we did learn? If we took, as our lesson, the failure of our efforts on a previous day and on a prior succession of days? If we saw our lives as what, in fact, they are: a series of grotesque mistakes, a catalogue of impostures and usurpations? W. shudders.

Why has it been left to him, rather than me, to face our disaster? I am a little more idiotic than he is, and therefore a little more forgetful. I can wake with a little more confidence in my labours; I can throw myself a little more obliviously into my studies (my so-called studies). And in that way, I throw myself ahead of him, too — ahead, and calling him after me by my power of forgetting, which is to say, my idiocy.

Why don't I learn?, W. asks himself. But he thanks God that I do not, and that I encourage him by my example.

'You need a woman in your life', says W. 'Why haven't you got a woman in your life?' Even Salomon Maimon, the *ragged philosopher*, had a girlfriend, and he never washed! Even Blanchot, the famous recluse, had Denise Rollin, though their relationship was largely epistolary. '*Dear Maurice...*'; '*Dear Denise...*'

W. tells me of the recently discovered love letters that Rosenzweig exchanged with the wife of his best friend. Margit Rosenstock — Gritli, as she was known — "*tore at his roots*", Rosenzweig wrote. But what of Gritli's husband? '*Eugen must know that he is the lord of our love, that it falls into an abyss if he turns away*', Rosenzweig wrote to Gritli. '*Before him we have to be revealed...*' They had to be revealed: there could be no secrets. Their love was so much more than mere adultery.

'*My soul encircles you and loves you*', Rosenzweig wrote to Gritli. '*This book I am now writing*' — he was writing the central section of *The Star of Redemption*, which concerns revelation — '*belongs to you. It is not "for you" but — yours. Yours — as I am*'.

'*Love is the binding of the human and the divine*': that's from *The Star of Redemption*, W. says. '*My experience of love, of being loved, my experience of God's command to love another, is itself divine*', that's what Rosenzweig wrote, W. says.

But what of Rosenzweig's friend Rosenstock, what did he think? And Rosenzweig's wife, who Rosenzweig had married in order to set up a real Jewish household after his return to Judaism: what was her opinion?

'Does Sal tear at *your* roots?', W. asks. 'Is Sal going to have to get a restraining order against you?' What did she say when I told her of Rosenzweig's love for his best friend's wife? — 'Don't get any ideas, fat boy!'

Then there was the romance between Kierkegaard and Regine, W. says. Kierkegaard knew almost as soon as he proposed to her, that he had made a mistake. But she'd said 'yes', and what was he to do now?

Kierkegaard wrote thirty-one letters in which he tried to make Regine realise how unsuited he was for marriage. '*You must understand I am subject to a higher calling...*'; '*A man must be allowed to rise to his true vocation...*' Kierkegaard sent her a book called *Old Memories,* and told her that she was already a thing of his past. And then he sent her his engagement ring, accompanied by a letter of farewell.

Regine '*fought like a lioness*', Kierkegaard wrote. And then, one terrible night, she confronted him and tore to pieces a little note he had written to her, which she carried in her bosom. — '*So you have played a terrible game with me*'. And then, '*Now I can bear it no longer; kiss me one last time and then have your freedom*'.

Kierkegaard was given his freedom, W. says, but freedom for what? To remember his love, and to revel in remembering. To intertwine his beloved with his published writings as in '*a secret arabesque*'...

Ah, it's typical gentile self-indulgence, W. says. Kierkegaard thought he was sacrificing his engagement in the name
of a higher cause, W. says. He didn't realise that Regine
was the higher cause! Kierkegaard thought the religious was
higher than the ethical, W. says. He didn't realise that the
basis of the ethical lies in the religious! Or is it the other way
round?

Sal is his higher cause, W. says. She's *our* higher cause! Ah,
what was he, before Sal?, W. says. He listened only to Mahler
and Gary Glitter, he remembers that. He wore white jeans and
espadrilles and '80s owl glasses. And if W. was a scholar back
then, he was a scholar without *heart*, a scholar who didn't
understand the *meaning* of scholarship, a scholar who understood nothing of what scholarship *honours*. He was a scholar
without a *higher cause*...

St. Hilda's College. We sit under the tree, a few of us, smoking. Žižek passes by. — 'So this is where they exile the smokers!' he cries.

Where's Žižek off to?, we wonder. He must have better things to do than hang around Oxford, we agree. He's probably going to see his wife, who's an Argentinean model, or something. A model-psychoanalyst. No, they got divorced, someone says.

We remember the photograph of Žižek and his model wife, taken the day they got married. It was circulated on the 'net. He looked hungover, regretful, vaguely surly. We felt he was one of us. How else would we look on our wedding day?

W. won't hear a word against Žižek, he says, although he hasn't read a line of Žižek's work. Žižek's what we all should be, W. says. He's a grafter, just as *we* should be grafters. He fills bookshelves with his publications, just as *we* should fill bookshelves with *our* publications. He's contracted diabetes from the sheer intensity of his thinking, just as *we* should contract diabetes from the sheer intensity of *our* thinking. He's working his way to exhaustion and early death, just as *we* should be working *our* way to exhaustion and early death.

W. knows why academics hate Žižek so much, he says. It's because Žižek's got their number. Žižek knows what he would have been had he not been banned from teaching by

Yugoslavian academia. He knows he would have been '*a poor stupid unknown professor from Ljubljana, probably dabbling in a little bit of this thinker, a little bit of that, a little bit of Marxism and so on*'. A poor stupid unknown professor just like all the other poor stupid unknown professors, just like all of us. A dabbler, writing on this and then that, lecturing on this and then that... oh God! Oh God!

Žižek's off, possessed by the most urgent of philosophical questions. But where are *we* going, who sit smoking under the tree? What possesses us, we dabblers, we poor stupid unknown idiots...?

What did Mladen Dolar, Žižek's old friend and comrade, tell us about *intellectual friendship*?, W. says. What, of his friendship with Žižek, Zupančič and the others; what, of his old associations with Mocnik and Bozovic when they combined to form the so-called *Ljubljana School of Psychoanalysis*?

That they began with friendship, and were sustained through friendship!, W. says. That they never departed from friendship in the face of Yugoslavian academia and the Yugoslavian state department. What chance did they have to get jobs, as they fell foul of the university authorities and the state authorities, and were unemployed for many years? What chance, as they aroused their managers' suspicion because of their interest in French thought, in *psychoanalytic* thought, and brought the luminaries of the French Lacanian School to Ljubljana?

They formed the *Journal for the Society of Theoretical Psychoanalysis* to publish one another, to support one another in thought, said Dolar. And in the end, what was the

Society of Theoretical Psychoanalysis? Nothing!, said Dolar. There was nothing going on at the centre, just him, Žižek and Zupančič drinking in a bar. It was the same with Žižek's series *Wo es War*, for Verso. There was no editorial board sitting in judgement, no solemn academic gatekeepers. It was a vehicle for Žižek to publish his Slovenian friends abroad!

Ah, how much we have to learn from the *Ljubljana School of Psychoanalysis*! How much, from *Wo es War*! Do we need to form a journal?, we wonder. Do we need to form a society? No: first of all, we need *friends!*, W. says. We need to *be* friends, don't I understand? And we need to have ideas!

Mladen Dolar was the real thing, we agree. The real Central European intellectual. — 'How do you think you looked when you sat beside him at that conference?', W. says. 'How do you think you came across, chairing his presentation?'

I was having a bad morning, I told W. later. But that didn't excuse it, W. says. A bad morning! — 'That question you asked...' He knew I was in trouble when Dolar finished reading, and the audience, taking in the many and rich ideas he had developed with exemplary grace and exemplary clarity, kept quiet. W. knew I was for it when it fell to me, Dolar's chair, to ask a question.

I could barely speak!, W. says. I babbled incoherently. I raved. — 'Everyone was hoping you'd stop'. But I didn't stop, did I? I carried on and on and on. Marx, this; Feuerbach, that. Some blousy-shirted idiot carrying on, W. says, and next to a real Central European intellectual...

Ah, how many times have I covered myself in shame, and by extension, covered him, W., in shame? How many times have I covered us both in shame? He'd been too stunned to *explain me* to Dolar, as he should have done, W. says. He — who should have known it would be necessary — simply wasn't ready to provide the usual excuses.

We're not going back into the conference, we decide. Žižek's gone, and why shouldn't we go? He'll follow me, W. says. I have a great instinct for escape, like a confined ape waiting for his keeper's inattention. At a moment's notice, I'll vault the walls...

W.'s ready to vault after me, he says. He's had enough! Isn't that why he keeps me with him: to be alongside another who has *had enough*?

But haven't I always had enough? Aren't I always demanding to leave? He's heard my whining in dozens of seminars, W. says. He's heard my mewling at every conference we've attended. I am, first of all, *a man of the outside*, W. says. A man who yearns to return to what lies beyond the walls...

The train northwest, heading to Manchester.

Hours pass. We're beginning to forget our pre-train lives. We're beginning to forget who we once were, out there, on the other side of the glass. But were we anything other than eternal voyagers? Were we anything other than children on a journey, amusing ourselves with our nonsense?

Trees in full leaf. Fields spreading out on all sides... The countryside is very lush, very beautiful, but W.'s in no mood to appreciate it. '*Nature is a corpse*', he quotes from Schelling. '*A veil of sadness is spread over all nature, a deep unappeasable melancholy*'.

Sometimes, he thinks it's time to get hold of his melancholy, W. says. To seize it by the scruff of its neck, and look at it in the face. But it's only *my* face, squirming and indolent, that would look back at him, W. says.

Is his melancholy deeper than his philosophy?, W. wonders; or is his philosophy deeper than his melancholy? He's never quite sure.

He's sure I bought my pink notebook just to annoy him, W. says. A pink notebook, with a pink ribbon as a bookmark, in which I write with a violet pen in violet ink, like a Japanese schoolgirl.

What have I been writing?, W. wonders, snatching it from my hands. Notes of our conversations? Stories of our adventures?

Ah, I've been *drawing*, W. says. He turns the page sideways. A kind of goat with wings and a star on its forehead. A goat with *breasts*, W. says. And what's this: a head with three faces?

Pages of minute writing, almost too small for the eye to see. It's a bit like Walser's *Microscripts*, W. says. It's a bit like the work of one of those *outsider writers*, which is discovered in mouldering piles in a flat somewhere. Ten thousand manuscript pages full of florid ravings, full of wild new mythologies...

'You really are the snack king, aren't you?', W. says, going through my rucksack. Is there any kind of snack I haven't brought with me? He admires me for it. There's something very *true* about my hunger, he says. Something telling.

W. picks up a pork scratching. Doesn't it look a bit like

Jesus?, he says. Actually, he thinks it looks a bit like me, being almost entirely made up of fat and gristle.

Ah, *Hello!* magazine, W. says, continuing his rummage. A special photospread of the Queen at Sandringham.

My attitude towards royalty is very surprising for a *man of the left*, W. says. Haven't I something of an obsession with the Queen? In airport queues and on long train journeys, he's heard me endlessly consider the question of whether I would accept an invitation to a royal garden party. Would I RSVP positively to an invitation signed in the Queen's hand? Of course I would, I decide on some occasions. Of course I wouldn't, on others.

W. puts aside my rucksack. — 'What are all these straps for? These zips?' Look at his man bag, he says. 'Do you see straps? Do you see zips? Do you see *Hello!* magazine?'

His man bag is an ark, W. says. He's carrying the most important ideas of Old Europe through the desert of Britain. But my rucksack is a trough, W. says. My rucksack is a *bucket of swill*.

W. flicks through his *New Scientist* special on climate change. The end of the world, spelt out in cold detail! He can't help but see the coming catastrophe in Biblical terms, W. says.

On the *first* day, God shaped heaven and earth from chaos, W. says, from that state which the Hebrew Bible calls the *tohu vavohu* — and darkness lay on the face of the deep. On the *second* day, dry land appeared, and put forth vegetation, the plants yielding seed, and the trees bearing fruit in which there was seed.

On the *third* day, the stars were born, and then the sun and the moon, each set in the firmament of the heavens to give light to the earth. On the *fourth* day, the waters brought forth swarms of living creatures, and birds flew across the sky.

On the *fifth* day, the beasts of the earth appeared, and then, on the *sixth* day, the first human being, made in the image of God. Be fruitful and multiply, was God's command. Fill the earth, and subdue it.

And on the *seventh* day, God rested from all his work which he had done, and saw that it was good. He saw the sleeping animals in their burrows, and the heads of corn bowing in the wind. He saw the grain elevators of the Canadian prairies, and the cattle of Newcastle Town Moor, grazing on the hills.

And was the Creation over then? The Creation was over, but the Destruction began.

On the *eighth* day, 'You appeared', W. says, 'scratching your head'. On the *ninth* day, I published my first book, and the heavens wept. And on the *tenth* day, I published my second book, and the stars fell from the sky.

On the *eleventh* day, our day, there are the storms of financial collapse, which are destroying the lives of the poor.

On the *twelfth* day, the rivers will dry up, and deserts will spread over the fields. The trees will wither, and the plants will no longer yield seed. The beasts of the earth will crawl, starving, on their bellies. The oceans of the world will toxify, and the very air will burn. The creatures of the waters will float in the waves, and the creatures of the air will flare from the skies.

On the *thirteenth* day, hurricanes will twist across the burning earth. The sea will darken, and turn black. The last human beings will gasp for breath. The earth will fall through darkness like a fireball.

On the *fourteenth* day, God will hang himself in heaven, despairing of his creation.

The plain of Manchester. That's how W. always thinks of it, the vista that opens as you come close to the city. As a great plain, stretching out in all directions. A plain that stretches *us* out. That leaves us prone beneath the enormous sky. Isn't that why Ian Curtis hanged himself: because he was stretched out beneath the enormous sky?

We are men of small cities, W. says. Cities you can cross in a day. Manchester is a massive city. An obscenely big city.

How did I put up with Manchester for all those years?, W. wonders. How come the city didn't get to me, destroy me? '*I wandered through that part of myself called Spain*', wrote Genet in *Thief's Journal*. I wandered through that part of myself called Manchester: isn't that how I thought of it?, W. says. Manchester is part of *me*, and not I a part of *it*: isn't that what I said to myself?

I had my bedsit, W. says. I drew the city around me like a cloak. And when I graduated, I stayed on the plain of Manchester, lost on that plain, a man without ambition, a man without significance. What did I think I was going to do? I was dreaming of *internal exile*, W. knows that. I was dreaming of going inside, and never coming out.

At Manchester Piccadilly, I'm bent over in agony. Too many snacks. My stomach...

'Your stomach is trying to save you', W. says. 'Don't you understand?' Only my viscera are honest, W. says. Only there, deep inside my body, buried under layers of fat, is there anything like honesty. In a way, it's comforting, W. says, the fact that there's a kind of *internal limit* to my idiocy, although it doesn't make me any easier to be around.

You're not going to get away with it, that's what my stomach says. *I'm not going to let you get away with it.* My stomach is my curse, W. says, and my judgement.

I think my stomach betrays me, W. says, when, in fact, my stomach, with its endless problems, its growling and grumbling, acts only in my interests.

That's why I look so bilious and green, W. says. And it's why we had to seek out an *emergency scheisse bar* when we visited Freiburg. *The emergency scheisse bar*: isn't that what we have to search out in *every* city, almost as soon as we arrive?

Manchester's completely changed, I tell W., as we walk from the station. I hardly recognise the place. When did it happen? *How* did it happen?

We must have been asleep. We must have forgotten that the world was changing. We've been outflanked, we agree. Outrun.

A new world appeared while we were napping. A new world of glass and steel, of *statement architecture*, in the years since I left the northwest. Look at the skyline! Look what they've done!

Beetham Tower has something, even he has to admit that, W. says. It looks like the future as we used to imagine it — the science fiction future, all streamlined and silvery. But the rest of it?

These are not our times, we agree. But whose times are they? The times of investors and financiers, we agree, of gentrifiers and speculators. The times of public-private partnerships and gated communities. The times of steel-balconied monuments to credit. The times of consumer-entrepreneurs, selling their soul to Capital and then buying it right back...

Even I'm outraged, W. says. He sees me climbing up Beetham Tower like King Kong, and him screaming in my fist like Fay Wray.

Neat Plymouth gins on ice by the canal, musing on our failure.

There are some thoughts that will be forever beyond us, W. says. The thought of our own stupidity, for example; the thought of what we might have been had we not been stupid. The thought of what *he* might have been, W., had he not been dragged down by the concrete block of my stupidity... The thought of what *I* might have been, had my stupidity simply been allowed to run its course... W. shudders.

Oh, he has some sense of what we lack, W. says. More than I have, but then he's more intelligent than I am. He has some sense that there's another kind of thinking, another *order of idea,* into which one might break as a flying fish breaks the surface of the water. He knows it's there, the sun-touched surface, far above him. He knows there are thinkers whose wings flash with light in the open air, who leap from wave-crest to wave-crest, and that he will never fly with them.

He lacks *brilliance*, that's his tragedy, W. says. There is a dimension of thought, another dimension of life, which he will never attain. The murk of his stupidity has a gleaming surface... He *half*-understands, *half*-knows; but he *doesn't* understand, he *doesn't* know.

But isn't that what saves him?, W. says. For if he had understood, really understood, how immeasurably he had failed, wouldn't he have had to kill himself in shame? If he had known, really known, the extent of his shortcomings, wouldn't his blood have had to mingle with the water?

Then again, if he really understood, he wouldn't *be* stupid, W. says. To know, really to know, would mean he had already broken the surface.

None of this troubles me, he knows that, W. says. Astray, that's what I've always been. Missing, in some sense. Absent without leave. — 'You're a deserter by inclination. You know nothing of loyalty, nothing of the cadre'. I'm not loyal to *philosophy*, W. says. I know nothing of it, the demand of thought.

'What are you interested in?', W. asks me. 'What, really? Because it's not philosophy, is it? It's not thought'. Still, I like *reading* about philosophy and *reading* about thought, that much is clear. It exercises some kind of fascination over me, W. says. There's something in me that responds. There's something that is left in me of the good and the true.

When do you *work*?', W. says. 'When do you have ideas?' But he knows the answer. I am too *busy* to work, I tell him. I am too *troubled* to have ideas.

I've been institutionalised, W. says. Bureaucratised! It was when I became the *perfect administrator* that I stopped doing any real philosophical work.

What do I do in my office?, W. asks. He knows the answer: go through emails. Fill out spreadsheets. Scour management communiqués with bloodshot eyes. And what do I do in the evenings? He sees me, in his mind's eye, W. says, opening a bottle of wine in the squalor of my flat, after a day at work. He sees me, booting up my laptop, getting ready to write.

But that's my problem!, W. says. I think that writing is the same as having ideas, when in reality, they are entirely different. You have to *stop writing* to have an idea, W. says. You have to pause and wait. Thought has to come to you, not you to it. You can't force thought by writing.

My writing is really the enemy of philosophy, W. says. Its waters close over the head of thought. Its dark matter occludes the sprawl of stars and planets. Sometimes he dreams that my non-thought is larger than thought, W. says. That it is *truer*, somehow. More in keeping with our times.

Of course, it's worse for me when I actually stop writing, W. says. It's worse when I collapse into my bed and try to sleep. He pictures me, staggering around my flat in the early hours, amidst the squalor, amidst the mould spores and the flies, preparing for bed. He sees me, drunk, or half drunk, on *Tesco's* cheapest wine, ranging around my flat like the abominable snowman, with my dressing gown flapping about me...

'You can never sleep, can you? You've never been able to sleep', W says. He sees me, lying sleepless in bed, full of great paranoid imaginings about the way I think they'll sack me. He sees me, lying there, quite panicked, fearing that I'll be sent back to the dole queue. And he sees me, falling asleep at last, collapsing into unconsciousness at last, just as dawn breaks, and the birds start singing, just as, at the opposite end of the country, W. is waking up, ready to begin his studies. He sees me, dreaming fitfully about *working out my notice* and *exit interviews*. He sees me, mouthing the words, No!,

No!, in my half-sleep... And he sees my eyes open again, the Leviathan awake, rolling out of my bed like a Spital Tongues Gargantua...

I take W. on a tour of my *emergency Scheisse toilets* in the city. The ones in the *Royal Exchange*, opposite the theatre they built within the vast interior of the building. The ones in the *Central Library*, in the basement beneath the many floors of books. The ones in the *House of Fraser*, on an underground corridor between different menswear departments. And I show him the secret toilet in *Waterstone*'s, hidden in a corner of the top floor.

W.'s impressed. A toilet for every part of the city centre. I left nothing to chance!

Manchester lacks a river, W. says. It lacks an expanse. That's why Mancunian thoughts are always *claustrophobic* thoughts, he says. It's why Mancunian thinkers are *constrained*, trying to fight their way free.

And there's the rain, brought by the terrible Westerlies, W. says. Manchester is particularly prone to Westerlies, which roll across its plain. The weather is so heavy here, W. says. So *crushing*.

The Mancunian thinker has constantly to struggle against melancholia, and thoughts of suicide, W. says. He thinks of Alan Turing, eating an apple he'd coated in cyanide. He thinks of Ian Curtis, hanging himself from the rope of a clothes-airer.

Sometimes, W. thinks that it's only the *destroyed thinker* who can press thought towards what matters most. That it's only *destroyed thoughts* that can think the whole. Is that why, despite everything, he reads my work so carefully? Is that why he still believes that I might have *something to say*?

There can be no thought from a *regenerated city*, W. says, as we look up at the warehouses converted into luxury flats. There can be no thought without dilapidation! No thought without *urban blight*!

Of course, I'm exactly the kind of person who would be drawn to Manchester, W. says. Exactly the type to make the *Mancunian mistake*.

I romanticised Mancunian despair, W. says. I didn't realise that Mancunian despair is only the desire to *leave* Manchester, the city in which I had just marooned myself in my error.

W. sees me as a young student, quite lost in Manchester. He sees me: a speck, an atom, rucksack on my back, trying to find my way around. Didn't I understand that the city was no place for me? That it was hard enough for those who belonged there?

What did I think I was doing? Whose life did I think I was leading? Did I think I could just become a man of the north? Did I think that northern despair had anything to do with *my* supposed despair? Did I think that the desolated landscapes of Manchester were the correlate of *my* supposed desolation?

The Mancunian soul is old and dark, W. says. The Mancunian soul has depths I cannot understand. Complexities! Did I think the Mancunian music that drew me to the city appeared from nowhere? Did I think Joy Division could happen *just like that*? Ian Curtis? Early New Order?

It is the poor who are the key to Manchester, W. says. The disenfranchised. The same people whose misery Engels documented, in his account of the city. Cotton workers spitting blood. Mill labourers with curved spines. Hollow-eyed children wandering among rubbish heaps...

Engels thought the poor would revolt, W. says. Hadn't Manchester been the city of protest? The city of Chartism? Ah, but the merchants of Manchester crushed the workers' movement. They massacred the protestors on the common land of St Peter's Field, and built the *Free Trade Hall* on the site of the massacre, mocking the dead, laughing at them. But Engels thought the north would rise again. He thought Manchester, the first city of the *industrial* revolution, would become the first city of the *workers'* revolution.

But the merchants of Manchester borrowed new models of *internal organisation* from the military — they borrowed *bureaucracy*, and the *chain of command*. The worker was encouraged to *defer gratification*, to develop *long-term goals* and *self-discipline*, in view of *future rewards*...

That's how the merchants of Manchester placed blinkers over the workers' eyes, W. says. That's how they placed a muzzle over the workers' mouths, and an iron collar around the workers' necks. And so Manchester became the Egypt of the workers' captivity. It became a *workhouse*, an open prison.

But Engels knew their end would come eventually, the merchants of Manchester, W. says. Capital is always greater than you, that's the lesson. Investors move elsewhere. Trade becomes unprofitable. Firms go out of business. Whole regions are ruined by *capital flight*...

The Mancunian textile industry was destroyed by foreign

competition. Its independent banks closed or relocated to London. Mass manufacturing became unprofitable, and mass unemployment arrived for good...

And Manchester fell asleep, W. says. The north had been broken, its industries destroyed. And Manchester lay down on its plain and slept. And as it turned in its sleep, Mancunian despair echoed in back-lane recording studios. As Manchester stirred uneasily, Mancunian horror sang on stage and record...

And idiots like me came to Manchester, didn't they?, W. says. Idiot-tourists, drawn by the depths of the Mancunian soul, by Mancunian melancholy. Idiots wandered among the derelict warehouses, and along the old viaducts and deserted towpaths. Idiots with their rucksacks came to live in the ruins.

'Think of what others might have achieved in your place', W. says. 'Think of what others might have done had they been given what you were given'. A desk. A computer. A set of bookshelves. And *time*, W. says. Above all: *time*.

I'm a usurper, aren't I?, W. says. I've taken the place someone else should have had. Someone cleverer than me, of course, W. says. More hard-working. Yes, he can picture it, W. says. Someone *slimmer* than me, dressed in a black shirt and black jeans. Someone *taller* than me, built like a missile of thought.

God knows, I've taken his place, too, W. says. I've taken *his* time. In fact, I've taken everyone's time, everyone who's had to listen to me, and, heaven forfend, to *read* me.

'Why do you write such bad books?', W. wonders, as he often does. Of course, it's a sign that something has collapsed that I can publish anything at all. Do I think I could have published something in the *old days?*, he says. Do I think I could have brought out a first book *and then a second book* when there were proper publishers and proper editors?

Ah, how did I slip past the gatekeepers? How did I slip a first book *and then a second book* past them? I thought I'd been cunning — I thought I'd been clever, W. knows that. Here's a chance, here's a niche, I thought. No one's looking, I thought. A doorway has opened, and if I just sneak through...

I thought I'd *seen an opportunity, W. says.* I thought I'd seen something no one else had seen: a chance, a possibility. I thought I'd *got one over on the world,* which in fact I hadn't. I thought I'd *stolen a march* on the *real* thinkers, the *real* writers, who were too busy procrastinating to *seize the day.*

Oh, they might be able to think, they might be able to write, but only I'm hungry enough, that's what I thought, isn't it? *Only I'm keen enough to see the situation for what it is, and take advantage of it,* that was it, wasn't it? *Only I'm desperate enough:* that's what I told myself. *I've been out in the cold so long,* I whimpered to myself. *I've suffered enough,* I wept to myself, and the tears glistened on my cheeks.

I was a member of the *real world,* that's what I thought, wasn't it?, W. says. I was in the business of marketing, of *self*-marketing, as you have to be in the real world, that's what I said to myself. And when there was an opportunity, when there was a chance to publish, why should I hold back?

I *knew* I was writing rubbish, that's what gets to him, W. says. I was gleefully writing rubbish, gleefully publishing rubbish... *They'll publish any old thing!,* I cried to myself. *They'll accept any old drivel!*

Shamelessness: that was it, W. says. I am a *shameless* man. *Let the others procrastinate, I have a book to publish,* I thought. *Let the thinkers think, let the writers write, but there's an opportunity here... I'm going to slip by unnoticed. I'm going to pass through the gates of publication like an opportunistic ninja...*

And I did, didn't I?: I slipped by unnoticed, W. says. No search lights found me. No klaxons went off, no SWAT teams appeared at my door, no snipers picked me off from rooftops. There was nothing — only eerie silence, as after heavy snow. Nothing — just metaphorical snowbanks, white and silent; just the metaphorical sky, white and silent. My first book was published — and nothing happened. My second book — and nothing happened.

'Even you, *even you* hoped you wouldn't get away with it', W. says. I wanted to be stopped! I wanted to be punished. I wanted my gleeful smile to be wiped from my face. — 'Something in you knows you've done wrong'.

A bad review: isn't that what I craved? Indignant emails from experts in my field. Letters of abuse from real scholars... To be told off, as by a stern but kindly headmaster. To be reprimanded, and then re-admitted to class. I wanted standards. I wanted punishment, W. says. I wanted *not to be able to get away with it*.

What I really wanted was to be shot down, W. says. To feel a hot bullet in my temple. To feel it cracking through my skull. I wanted to be cut down by machine gun fire. I wanted to be bayoneted and collapse in the snow, W. says. He sees it in his mind's eye: my dying face with a smile that says, *justice has been done...*

But in truth, there's no one to offend, not any more, W. says. There are no sentries at the gate. No one cares. It's collapsed — isn't that what I've taught him?, W. says. The academic system's collapsed. Academic publishing's collapsed. My book — and the millions of other books, there being more books published now than ever before — meet with perfect silence, perfect indifference. The university's finished, and we're in outer space, tumbling head over heels into the darkness.

My Manchester was Old Hulme, of course, W. says. Old, unregenerated Hulme, with its low-rise crescents, system-built in the '60s and now condemned and nearly deserted. My Manchester was *Hulme Free State*, which had made squats out of the maisonettes of stained concrete.

That was my bohemian phase, W. says. My-living-like-a-hippie-phase. Only I could never live like a hippie, could I? I could never live like the crusties and ravers around me...

I was a *failed bohemian*, W. says, living rent free in my squat, with colour photocopies of Hindu gods blu-tacked up on my wall. I was a *botched communalist*, avoiding my flatmates, emerging from my room only in the early hours, and skulking along the decks so I wouldn't be seen.

You would have thought that a half-Dane would be stirred by egalitarian ideals, of sharing possessions and resources, of group decisions and non-hierarchical structures, W. says. You would have thought that a half-Dane would be well prepared for communal life: for cooking together and cleaning together and planning socially-minded activities together.

How long was it before the *failed bohemian* broke the house rules?, W. wonders. How long before my squatmates were muttering and grumbling about my inability to clean, my general squalor? How long before they realised that I was *utterly incapable of communal living*?

reason, Kierkegaard saved me. *Either/Or*: that was the book I came across in an Old Hulme jumble sale, I've told him that. *Either/Or*: that was the book which awoke me from my *bohemian slumbers*.

Of course, my type usually lose themselves in conspiracy theories and books about UFOs, W. says. My type usually lose themselves in the collected works of Colin Wilson, or in Dennis Wheatley's Library of the Occult. So why Kierkegaard? What was it about *Either/Or*?

Was it the infinite variations on the expression of despair of A., the pseudonymous author of the first part of Kierkegaard's book, that impressed me?, W. wonders. Was it A.'s pages of lamentations? Or was it the call-to-arms of B., the pseudonymous author of the second part of Kierkegaard's book, that spoke to me? Was it B.'s exhortations to *look at oneself in the mirror*?

Either a life mired in shit, or a life of *thinking* about a life mired in the shit: isn't that the choice *Either/Or* presented me with?, W. says. And so shit began to think about itself, W. says. Shit looked at itself in the mirror...

I read *Philosophical Fragments* as gangs of Hell's Angels fought outside over drug deals, I've told W. I read the *Concluding Postscript to the Philosophical Fragments* as I heard gunshots in Woodcock Square. I read *Repetition* in the laundrette, and *Fear and Trembling* as I queued for patties in *SamSam*'s.

I zigzagged across the greens to avoid the marksmen, with my copy of *Stages on Life's Way*, didn't I? I cracked open

Playing Jandek on the shared stereo... did I think that would bind everyone together?, W. says. Tacking Louis Wain prints to the living room walls... did I think that would produce *fellow feeling*? My endless insomniac pacing... did I believe that would endear me to my new squatmates? And, worst of all, the dreadful sight of me when I rose in the morning, rolls of fat visible through the holes in my dressing gown: why should anyone have to see that?

I'm not *socialised*. That's the problem, W. says. I'm not *housebroken*. But there I was, W. says: the *failed bohemian*, trying everyone's patience. Didn't I singlehandedly destroy my commune? Didn't the *failed bohemian* drive away all his fellow squatters? I was a living reminder, for them, of how far Old Hulme had fallen. I was the living embodiment of the forces that were destroying Squat City.

But in truth, everyone was leaving, W. says, I've told him that. Trouble had come to the crescents: travellers with pit-bulls, French skinheads, rumoured to be on the run for murder, junky casualties of rave culture, ready to stab you with a syringe for loose change.

Armagideon: someone painted that on a crescent wall, I've told W. *Sky is burnin*: someone painted that across the boarded-up health-food shop. *Blood inna fyah*: across the metal shutters pulled down over *PSV*. *Earth a run red*: sprayed across the windshield of a crusty van.

He feels sorry for me, in a way, W. says. I was too late for *real* counter-culture. I was too late for the rebellions of the '80s, in which he had a part, W. says. I was too late for *politics*...

A few years earlier, and I might have taken part in the Poll Tax riots, W. says. A few years earlier, and I would have lived through the glory days of Old Hulme, when sound systems would reverberate from the roofs, and ravers would come from all over the city to the nightclub they'd made by jack-hammering through maisonette walls.

But now the *failed Bohemian* was one of the last men of Old Hulme, W. says. One of the last residents, along with the Rastas, wandering the empty decks.

The squat became damper. Colder. The walls were blackening. The electricity was cut off. There was no more hot water... The smell of rotting rubbish was overwhelming. Fires burned everywhere on the decks. Packs of half-wild dogs ran on the greens.

Who did I imagine I was?, W. says. What fantasy was I living? What film was playing in my head?

'How on earth did you come across Kierkegaard in Old Hulme?', W. asks. 'And why Kierkegaard, of all thinkers?'

In our time — and this is an indictment of our time — a figure like Kierkegaard becomes a magnet for all kinds of lunatics, W. says. That's how it was for me, wasn't it, in the middle of Old Hulme? First came my obsession with Kafka, which launched me towards my undergraduate studies. Then came my obsession with Kierkegaard — which launched me, *threw* me, towards my *post*graduate studies. But why Kierkegaard?

Internal exile. That was my solution to the problem of Britain, wasn't it?, W. says. To carry out an internal correlate of the great external voyages of Joyce and Beckett, of Flusser and Gombrowicz. I was going to go *inward*, just as they went *outward*. I was going to discover a Paris of the soul, a South America of the mind.

Expect nothing from the world!, I said to myself, didn't I? Sit life out! Go on the dole! On the sick! Claim to be seeing things! Hearing things! Claim to be in the grip of imaginary mental illnesses! Get yourself committed! Locked up! Dream away your life in a serene captivity!

But then there was Kierkegaard, W. says. Then, for some

the spine of *The Concept of Irony* as my breath froze in the air in my sunless back room. I began *The Concept of Anxiety* as I stamped my feet for warmth by a fire of old plywood on an upper deck. And I filled notebooks with my thoughts on *The Writing Prefaces* and *The Book on Adler,* while muggers waited in dark corners, with their Stanley knives and screwdrivers.

Did I bother the rastas about Kierkegaard? W. wants to know. He can imagine it, he says. He sees it in his mind's eye: the *failed bohemian* talking about Kierkegaard to the rastas. Did I bother the crusties about Kierkegaard? W. can see that as well, he says. The *failed bohemian* blathering about Kierkegaard to the crusties. And what about the junky ravers — did I bother them? He can see that, too, W. says: bug-eyed ravers staring blankly at the *failed Bohemian* chattering about Kierkegaard...

Oxford Road. W. fans himself with his copy of *The Star of Redemption*. Manchester is so *humid*, he says.

We head to the cool of the Manchester Museum. Dark halls of mummies. Preserved insects pinned on display boards. On the top floor, I show W. the living wasps' nest in a box of glass: a slice of honeycombed nest, with wasps crawling all over it.

But W. is only interested in reading the plaques about Egyptian mythology. About the beasts of chaos depicted in the mausoleums of the pyramids: hybrid creatures, half frog, half bat; mad dogs and storm-demons; flying vipers and scorpion-men. He reads about Apep, the *evil* god, their three-headed, six-eyed leader, who could neither see nor hear. And about the *cry* of Apep, because that's all Apep did, W. says: cry and lament his own existence, as he slithered through the primordial darkness.

I tell W. about the three-headed, six-eyed dragon that Indra defeats in Indian mythology. And about the three-headed, six-eyed dragon that Marduk kills in Iranian mythology. I tell him about the monsters of Indian mythology: of Snavidka — who boasted that when he reached adulthood, he would take heaven and earth as his chariot. And I tell him of Gandarva, the dragon of the sea, who threatened to blow out the stars and swallow the sun...

Paganism!, W. cries. Heathenism! These are the monsters Judaism sets to flight. In some ways, they remind him of the beasts the prophet Daniel sees, in his visionary dream, W. says. A lion with eagle's wings... a bear-like blob... a four-headed leopard... And then, the *fourth* beast of Daniel's dream, the most terrible of all, with its ten horns, and an eleventh one sprouting from its back, with a tiny mouth and tiny eyes, screaming that it is about to turn the world into a *waste of desolation.*

Of course, the beasts are only personifications of the tyrants, W. says. Of the Seleucid Empire. Of the Babylonian invaders. They are ways of talking about the destructive element of the last days, before God's justice prevails. Before salvation comes, the forces of chaos will rage as never before: doesn't the Bible tell us that? Before redemption comes, before God reigns on earth, there will be a period of terrible tribulation: that's what Daniel sees in his vision, W. says.

Sometimes W. wants to send up a great cry of dereliction. Not his dereliction, he says, but dereliction in general. Abandonment.

Who has abandoned us? Who has left us behind? Who left us to ourselves, and left him to me? Who thrust me into his arms like a foundling?

The times are changing, W. says. A whole epoch is ending. He fears that we are its gravediggers, W. says. That the pit we have dug for ourselves — the disaster of our careers, the ludicrous posturing of our lives as thinkers — is the tomb into which philosophy itself will be lowered...

Plato is turning in his grave, W. says. Kant is spinning in his grave. Did Cohen see what was coming? Did Cassirer?

The apocalypse has always been our alibi, our excuse, W. says. The greatest of sick-notes. What we could have done, if the end hadn't seemed so close!

Of course, the apocalypse was also the *condition* of our thought, W. says. Why else have we felt such an urgency to think? Why else has our thinking been so marked by despair?

We were born of the apocalypse to think the apocalypse,

W. concludes. We are only the way the apocalypse has come to know the nightmare of itself. Because apocalypse does suffer from itself, W. says.

The apocalypse doesn't *want* to be the apocalypse, that's the thing, W. says. That's why we should pity it, and pity ourselves, as the ones in whom the apocalypse has awoken to self-awareness. And that's why W. should pity me, who am so much closer to the apocalypse than he is.

My insomnia is only the insomnia of apocalypse, W. says. My obesity is only the obesity of apocalypse. And my idiocy is only an apocalyptic idiocy, a way for the apocalypse to say, *end me now!*

'*What else does this craving, and this helplessness proclaim*',
W. reads from his notebook, '*but that there was once in man a true happiness, of which all that now remains is the empty print and trace?*'

True happiness: what can this possibly mean for W.?
What sense of it can he have? I've been in his life too long, he says. Far too long, blocking the sun of what might have been his happiness with the great round moon of my stupidity.

Ah, the lunar eclipse of his life! The obliteration of his hopes and dreams! He knows his happiness, what he might have been, only from the faint glow of its corona.

We're growing old, W. says. Our eyes are dulling and our hair is greying. Even *my* eyes, the one who he took as a protégé! Even *my* hair, the one he singled out for being so young!

Socrates taught Plato, W. says. Plato taught Aristotle. And Aristotle taught Alexander, who conquered half the world. Hasn't W. dreamt of a pupil who would leap ahead of him? To be superseded in thought... To become a kind of *springboard* for a thinker who would leap yet higher, yet farther... To nurture the protégé who would *blast new skies open...*

But he has engendered only a *monster of thought*, W.

says. The Biblical Beast with blood on its muzzle. Something Hindu, with thirty-seven heads.

What is my significance?, W. wonders. Do I illustrate some broader trend? Am I a man *of* our times, or *against* our times? Sometimes, he thinks I am *ahead* of our times, W. says. That I am a kind of prophetic witness. That I am a *living sign*, such as you might find in the Bible.

W. thinks of the later prophets, who no longer speak with God as Moses and Abraham did — as with a neighbour, face to face, or as the Bible says, *mouth to mouth*. He thinks of the prophets who God commanded to *incarnate* the message they were charged to deliver.

Isaiah was told to wander naked and barefoot for three years, in order to send a message to the King of Assyria, to parade his prisoners naked and barefoot to shame Egypt. God told Jeremiah to make wooden yokes and put them on his neck, and, when a false prophet broke them, to replace them with yokes of iron, in order to send a message that Israel will not put its neck under the yoke of Babylon...

But I was a prophet who didn't know that he was a prophet, W. says. I was a sign who didn't know what he signified. Which made *his* role very clear, W. says. Which made it obvious what *he* was put on earth to do...

Philosophy gives substance to our suffering, W. says. Philosophy gives sense to suffering by communicating it to others. Speech, the capacity to speak: that's what overcomes futility, W. says. That's what does combat with the senselessness of the world.

And W. was going to let *me* speak! That was his role,

he says. He was going to hear the suffering of the world as it resounded through me. He was going to decipher my bellowing. The Jew in him would *redeem* the Hindu in me, W. says. His Catholic atheism would redeem my Protestant atheism. He would bring fruit trees to my waste, and calm to my troubled waters...

But W. didn't understand that it could be the other way round: that the Hindu in me could rise up against the Jew in him. That my Protestant atheism could wrestle his Catholic atheism to the ground! He didn't see that I was on the same side as Apep, or Snavidka, or Gandarva, of the beasts of the desert and the beasts of the sea. He didn't see that I was on the same side as the *tohu vavohu*, as welter and waste.

A study morning in Chetham's Library. We examine the plaque commemorating Marx's and Engels' visit. It was here they realised that Marx was of '*superior analytical skill*', the plaque says. Here, they decided that Marx should have as much time as he needed to research the overthrow of capitalism, and that Engels should work to support him.

Which one of us has '*superior analytical skill*'?, W. wonders. Which one should give up his job and devote himself to research the overthrow of capitalism in our time? The answer is obvious, W. says: *I* should work to maintain *him*, as he researches contemporary problems of political economy. Imagine what he could accomplish, with all the time in the world! Imagine what he would write!

But sometimes, W. thinks that he should support me, allowing me to write *my* masterpiece, he says. Oh I won't write a *Capital*, he knows that, W. says. I'll barely manage to form a sentence. But my work will have a *symptomatic* value that will exceed anything he could write, W. says. Nothing to do with its content. It's the *fact* of it that will be significant, W. says. Its monstrosity.

Of course, I could just print out the pages of my blog, and bind them between hard covers, W. says. That would be enough. But how could my blog be contained between hard covers? My blog is infinite, W. says. It's an example of the *bad* infinite, as Hegel would call it. The *spurious* infinite... It just goes on and on...

Writing falling into itself, W. says. Lost in itself. Wandering its own corridors. Writing that has forgone the power of signification. Abyssal writing, in which the whole world is lost, and loses itself over and again... Writing that obliterates the very face of God...

W. snaps shut the copy of Josiah Thompson's *Kierkegaard* that he found on the library shelves. We should shun Kierkegaard scholarship, he says. Kierkegaard scholarship can only make us afraid to do what we must do: remake Kierkegaard in our image. We must be free to dream, as he has dreamt, of a Kierkegaard who was happily married to Regine, W. says. Of a Kierkegaard who understood that the religious sphere is no higher than the ethical one, and that love for God is really love for the other person. Hasn't W. dreamt of a Kierkegaard who never believed that Jesus was really the Messiah, or that messianism could ever be understood in terms of the coming of a particular person? Of a Kierkegaard who had faith only in the *messianic epoch*?

His Kierkegaard is turned to the world, W. says. To politics! His is a Kierkegaard of the barricades, whose despair has caught fire, whose inwardness has become outwardness, whose *religious* faith has become *ethical* faith, has become *political* faith.

What is my Kierkegaard like, W. wonders. How many *arms* does he have? How many *heads*? Does my Hindu Kierkegaard *dance*? Hindu deities are always dancing, W. says.

The best Kierkegaard is the *last* Kierkegaard, W. says, the Kierkegaard who has curdled and lost all moderation. We, too, must let ourselves curdle and lose all moderation, W. says. Just as Kierkegaard called his opponent a *glob of snot*, we must call our opponents *globs of snot*, W. says. Just as Kierkegaard called the entirety of Christendom an *invention of Satan*, we must understand the entirety of Britain as an *invention of Satan*. Why don't I see the extremes to which we must go?

Whitworth Park. Sometimes W. imagines we might *walk* our way to ideas, he says, as we wander through the trees. That to walk — if we walked far enough, hard enough — might also be to *think*. Or at the very least, to think *about* thinking. To have ideas *about* ideas, ideas about the ideas we might one day have.

But I'm no walker, that's the problem, W. says. Not anymore. Was I ever a walker?, W. wonders. Did he only imagine us walking together? Our walks to Cawsand, through Mount Edgcumbe, our walks to Whitley Bay, through Tynemouth and Cullercoats... He's not sure anymore, W. says.

Of course, he's a man of the *promenade*, W. says. He walks slowly, his torso held erect, looking all about him. He's *interested* in the world, W. says, open to surprises! Not like me, who am always bent over, always looking at the space on the pavement immediately in front of my feet.

And I walk so quickly!, W. says. What am I trying to escape? — 'Yourself? Well, in that case, you're doomed'. Once, he and Sal saw me from afar, a pedestrian among pedestrians. They saw me just as a stranger might see me: as a derelict, walking at a furious rate, head down, glowering. What's wrong with that man?, they wondered to each other. What's his problem? And then they saw it was me, and they know all about my problems.

There's a fundamental difference in our *philosophy of walking*, W. says. He is a *Jewish* walker, for whom every walk is an exodus, a leaving behind of the house of bondage. For the Jew, every walk is a *political* act, a determined effort to found a new community, to journey together away from the captivity of Egypt.

But I am a *Hindu* walker, W. says, for whom walking is not political, but only ever *cosmological* — 'You set out to come back again! You go forth only to return!'

The Hindu walks in circles, W. says, as in the cycle of rebirth, or the turning of the Four Ages. But the Jew has only one direction. The Jewish walker is always walking towards Canaan.

Eid in Rusholme, on the curry mile. Barriers free the street from cars. Families walk out to celebrate the end of Ramadan. Women with hennaed hands. Men in white prayer robes. Children shouting and running. Is this what it will be like after the revolution?

He feels attuned to Indian *pathos*, W. says. To Indian *joy*! The chaos! The colours! The smells! And everyone out, walking together. The people joyfully wandering in the streets. He thinks of what he's read about Ghandi's Indian revolution. About the *Quit India* movement. About *Non-Cooperation*. Didn't Ghandi bind the Indians into a single, interwoven community? Didn't he mobilise Hindus and Muslims alike — and the Sikhs, the Jains, taking no heed of old enmities...?

He's always understood me to be a kind of *Bartleby* of politics, W. says. *I would prefer not to*: that's what my indifference to social questions amounts to. Or, better: *Fuck off, I'm eating*.

I'm *antisocial*: that much is clear, W. says. *Reclusive*. He's seen the expression on my face during long conference presentations. He's seen the wild desire for freedom that burns in my eyes. I want to leap over the walls! To bellow! To scream! And doesn't he want to escape with me, a whelk on the side of a whale?

He remembers our great conference break-outs, W. says. To Titisee, from Freiburg University, paddling out onto the lake. To the bar at Five Points, in Nashville, from Vanderbilt University, demanding Plymouth Gin. To the *Rendezvous Barbecue*, from the University of Memphis, wanting only the finest ribs… Outside!, I cried, W. recalls. I want to *breathe!*, I cried. Air!, I bellowed. He loved me in those moments, W. says. Everything that was good and noble in me shined forth.

I find the company of academics intolerable, W. says. Unbearable! And isn't he the same? Doesn't he share something of my dread, and my urge to flee? Isn't he also becoming something of an *academic savage*?

But there are other kinds of people, W. says, that's what I have to understand. Other ways of being together. Political friendship: do I have any sense of that? Of what it means to band together against a common enemy? Of what it means to share a commitment, to be part of collective work, free from all personal ambition?

W. reminds me of what Tronti wrote of the early days of *operaismo*:

> *We brought together a fine old madhouse. During our meetings, we would spend half our time talking, the rest laughing. For us, the classic political friend/enemy distinction was not just a concept of the enemy, but a theory and practice of the friend as well. At that moment, another world was possible. I've never yet met people of higher human worth.*

Political joy; political laughter, W. says: can I imagine that?

We stop for Indian snacks. Chevda. Murukku: I know all the names, W. says.

Kierkegaard was a man of the street, W. says. At home, Kierkegaard rarely opened his door to anyone. But on the streets, where he walked every day, his high-shouldered, crab-like gait familiar to everyone...

Contemporary accounts have him walking arm in arm will all kinds of people: politicians and actors, poets and philosophers, bakers and fruit-sellers, market porters and bar-women. And didn't Kierkegaard like to go out on the stagecoach to the country, to feel the sun on his face and speak to the farmers in their fields? Didn't he stand out in the barns and chat with the herdsmen, and sit out by the road with the stone breakers?

But when a satirical review published caricatures of him, Kierkegaard became a laughing stock to his fellow Copenhageners. Children followed him, shouting out the title of his first book: '*Either/Or, Either/Or!*' His former walking companions sniggered...

And so Kierkegaard went inside, closing his doors against the world. His inwardness went unchecked. He became paranoid, raving... faith festered inside him. His belief went sour! He was dying of ridicule! Dying of loneliness! Poor Kierkegaard! *Poor Søren!*, as they called after him in the street. *Poor Søren!*

And what did they call after me in the street, when I lived in Rusholme?, W. asks. What did the children shout after me, as I passed? Ah, but he knows I hid myself from everyone, then as now. I barely left my bedsit, except to go for my evening kebab. To be is to be perceived, Berkeley said. But who perceived me?, W. wonders. Only a god or a beast can be alone, according to Aristotle, W. says. Was I god or beast?, W. wonders.

Manchester, stranded on a rush-hour bus. We rank our friends in order of their intelligence. Then we rank them in order of their melancholia, and wonder if there's a correlation. Then we rank them according to their *punctuality*, cross-referencing our results with our previous findings.

Our brighter friends are always late, we decide, always disorganised. Our brighter friends are also melancholy, which is probably why they can never keep their appointments. How many times have they left us standing, looking at our watches? W. always smiles on such occasions. — 'There are more important things than meeting us', he says. 'Much more important things!'

If anything, I am *too* punctual, W. says. I'm always there before everyone, anxiously pacing about. What do I think I'm going to miss?

I have a dim sense that something is going to happen — but what? What can I possibly understand of what is going to happen? You can't replace intelligence with punctuality, W. says.

Our Manchester friends are late, very late. We should pay it

no heed, W. says, over our pints in the bar. We should culti-
vate the *art of waiting*.

But it's no good. By the time our friends arrive, fresh from
the gym and in their cycling lycra, we are already drunk, and
speaking in great apocalyptic gusts. Before long, we're alone
again, having driven our friends away into the night.

'No one wants to talk to us, have you noticed that?', W.
says. 'We're like lepers in the middle ages. Someone might as
well be walking in front of us, ringing a bell'.

'You shouldn't have told them about the *spider people*',
W. says. 'That's what did it'. The spider people. Our pheno-
types are being disrupted, I'd told our Manchester friends. It's
the increase in *carcinogens* and *tertogens*, I'd said. The rise in
allergens and *hormone disrupters*.

Impairment will be the norm, I'd said. Vestigial limbs.
The spider people will appear, with their four or five or six
spare limbs flailing uselessly in the air.

They'll be very gentle, the spider people, I'd told our
Manchester friends. Very vulnerable. Which means they'll be
set upon at once, their useless limbs pulled off one by one.
They'll be mocked and killed. And probably *eaten*, I'd said,
since there'll be nothing to eat in the new world. Nothing to
eat except spider people.

I drove away our friends, W. says. Futurology and friendship do not mix.

My monk years, W. says. It's the most mysterious of episodes to him. What drove me to the monks, or, stranger still, the monks to me?

How did I, who had no religious belief, no experience of religion, no understanding of religion, end up living among monks as their guestmaster? How did I, out of all the other candidates — and there must have been other candidates, other monk hangers-on, who would have wanted my role — become guestmaster to a community of monks?

Oh, he knows the story, W. says. It was Kierkegaard that led me there, that's what I told him, wasn't it? It was Kierkegaard that made me seek sanctuary during the regeneration of Manchester.

I'd been called to the Job Centre, W. remembers my telling him that. They were hunting us down, the long-term unemployed, the long-term sick. It was time for us to be straightened out and reskilled. Time for flipcharts and group-work and IT training for the new reality.

We were to learn about our *transferrable skills*, I've told W. We were to learn about *personal branding*. We were to learn about *time management* and *planning and organisation*. We were to learn about *working well with others*, and *forming good working relationships*. We were to learn about *motivation* and *enthusiasm*, about *showing initiative* and being *self-starting*. We were to learn about *sharing a firm's mission...*

And isn't that what drove me to the monks?, W. says. Wasn't it in panic that I banged at the monastery gates, and waved my Kierkegaard books in their faces? Save me from the regenerators! Save me from back-to-work training!

But why did the monks take me in? If Dostoevsky had holy fools, W. says, I was an *un*holy fool: A Prince Myshkin without humility; an Alexei Karamazov without goodness; a Saul who never converted; a Judas *after* his act of betrayal; a Thomas who did nothing but doubt...

Maybe they were testing their spiritual strength, W. says. Maybe they meant to sharpen the edge of their faith along the whetstone of my *un*faith. Maybe I was their wilderness, their desert, their devil of temptation. By bringing me close, maybe they sought to bring themselves closer to the presence of God. Maybe it was their effort to *force* the Messiah.

He sees me in his mind's eye, W. says. He sees the *unholy fool,* standing between the monks and the world, admitting guests, showing them up to their rooms which he had carefully readied, preparing lunch and dinner for them. He sees me, W. says, although he doesn't understand what he sees: the *monastery idiot,* making beds and running his cloth along the dado, taking the coats and hats of ecclesiastical callers, making pleasantries in the oak-parqueted reception room. He sees me, W. says, the *community divvy*, arm in arm with a monk he's escorting across the icy pavement. He sees me, the *monastery imbecile,* sitting in attendance at ecumenical dinners, smiling on nut-brown Copts, and calling taxis for white-robed Dominicans heading back to the station.

How it confuses W., for whom the story of my life,

otherwise, is relatively clear. The monks took me in: but why? why me? What recommended *me* to *them*? What, when I had no idea of what *living a spiritual life* might mean?

Of course, he too has lived with monks, W. says. Over a long summer on Caldey Island, he even thought of becoming one. But, as always on this topic, W. says nothing more. I'd jot it all down in my notebook, he says, and put it all up on the 'net. A veil must be drawn over some things, W. says. A kind of silence must be observed — and W. took a vow of silence, back when he was thinking of joining the Trappists.

'There are moments in one's life ... ah, how can you explain it to an idiot?', W. says, with particular fervour. 'Sometimes, you're vouchsafed something... Sometimes...' No, no, he won't try and explain, he says.

And isn't that where it began, W.'s real sense of religion, of religiosity, which has nothing to do with sighing after a world beyond this one? Isn't that where he understood that the question of religion wasn't to be left with philosophers and metaphysicians, and addressed in terms of *philosophical* and *metaphysical* conceptions of religion?

He was silent, W. says. He spent whole days in solitary prayer. In the time between services, when they were allowed to converse, he would wander the beach with an older monk, a proper holy man, meditating upon faith and upon the essence of religion, W. says.

'What does "God" mean?', W. asked the holy man, like a child. 'What is religion?' Sometimes you have to ask the simplest questions, W. says. And the answers he received...? No, he won't tell me, W. says. He won't breathe a word.

Some conversations change everything, W. says. It's not the *content* of what is said. Nor is it a matter of intensity. Seriousness, yes. That's essential. *Absolute* seriousness. But seriousness can be *light!*, W. says. Speaking seriously can be ease itself! His time with the older monk was spent in easy conversation, W. says. They talked about ordinary things, concrete things. All really profound conversations are about ordinary things, W. says.

Opposite the university, under the motorway bridge. A junkie in a sky-blue jumper asks for money for *chippies*. W. scrutinises him closely as he gives him some change. — 'You can never be sure', W. says. 'He might have been a *ragged philosopher*'.

I quiz W. on the strange superstitions of the *former Essex postgraduates*. Is it really true that you have to leave your back door open in case a former associate raps on your window? Is it really true that a place must always be left at your table, in case a former Essex postgraduate arrives unbidden for a meal? But W. keeps quiet.

I ask W. whether it's true that there is a secret fund into which the more solvent former Essex postgraduates pay, and upon which their poorer fellows might draw. I ask whether the rumours are true about the *University in Hiding*, to which all the former Essex postgraduates belong. Are there really secret handshakes and secret winks — certain signs that allow one former Essex postgraduate to recognise another, even though they may never have met at their alma mater? Was W. looking for a secret wink from the junkie in the sky-blue jumper?

Ah, how can he explain it to me, what it means to be a former Essex postgraduate?, W. wonders. How can he make me understand?

W. recalls the legend of Chouchani, the Talmudic master who taught both Levinas and Weisel. No one knows where Chouchani was born, W. says. No one knows where he grew up. No one knows where he acquired his immense learning, which did not concern only Judaism and Jewish matters, but mathematics, too, and philosophy, and the arts. He spoke all the living languages of Europe, W. says, and a few dead ones besides.

Chouchani lived like a tramp, W. says, unkempt, wandering, staying for a while with those he took as his pupils, before moving on. And you had no choice about Chouchani taking you as his pupil, W. says. *He* selected *you*, not you him! He'd bang on your window; he'd demand to be admitted to your home. And there he would stay, night after night. There, demanding nothing but attention to the intellectual matters at hand. Nothing but study, and seriousness in study. And then, just like that — did he think you'd learnt enough? did he suppose you'd reached your limits? — he disappeared. Just like that, he was gone, his room cleared — disappeared. Chouchani was the Mary Poppins of Talmudic studies, W. says.

We can trace Chouchani's path, W. says. New York. Strasbourg. Jerusalem. And didn't he die in Montevideo? Isn't it in Uruguay that his tombstone can be found, and on it, the lines, 'His birth and his life are bound up in a secret'?

Think of Chouchani's mastery of the Bible!, W. demands. Bring to mind Chouchani's knowledge of the two Talmuds, the Midrash, the *Zohar* and the work of Maimonides!, W. exhorts. Contemplate his mastery of the latest theories from mathematics, and from physics, and his total knowledge of literature, ancient and contemporary, and his boundless philosophical learning!

And now, W. says, imagine an *entire generation of thinkers* who rose to these heights! Imagine an *entire generation* of Essex postgraduates in whom thought was burning as brightly as that!

How *harsh* he was, Chouchani!, W. says. And how harsh they were with one another, the Essex postgraduates! How merciless in debate Chouchani was!, W. says. But the Essex postgraduates were merciless, too; they, too, would let nothing pass! How *serious* the great Talmudist was!, W. says. But the Essex postgraduates, too, were serious! Thought, to them, was always a *matter of life and death!*

Did Chouchani hold a knife to the throat of one of his pupils, who was slow to understand the repercussions of Tossafot's commentary?, W. wonders. Well, a knife was held to *his* throat in Essex University Student Union Bar, he says, because of some misunderstanding or another on his part, some obtuseness about the B-deduction in Kant's *Critique of Pure Reason*, or about the syntheses of time in Deleuze's *Difference and Repetition*. Rightly so!, W. says. He needed to be taught a lesson. He needed to learn!

And didn't W. in his turn, hold a knife to the throats of younger Essex postgraduates? W. should hold a knife to my throat, he says. Not because I would be capable of reaching the same intellectual heights as an Essex postgraduate, W. says. But to give me an *idea* of what it meant to be an Essex postgraduate.

That's another superstition: that every former Essex postgraduate keeps a knife in the house at all times, blade sharpened. A knife that might be used against them if they become a *betrayer of thought*, or that they might use on one of thought's betrayers. I'd better watch it when I visit him, W. says.

Manchester was good to us, W. says, as we wait for our train, back at Piccadilly Station. It *was* good. We gave our talk, fielded questions, we didn't get lynched...

Capitalism has triumphed, W. told our audience. Capitalism has conquered the *external* world, and now it's going to conquer the *internal* one, too. *The very intimacy of our lives*, that's capitalism's new frontier, W. said. Our private ideas, our tastes, our *moods*: that's what capitalism has set out to conquer now.

In the end, our loves and friendships will become *capitalist* loves and *capitalist* friendships, W. told our audience. Our innermost hopes and dreams will become *capitalist* hopes and *capitalist* dreams. Our sighs will become *capitalist* sighs. Our wistfulness, *capitalist* wistfulness. Even our philosophy, opposed as it is to capitalism in every way, will become *capitalist* philosophy! W. said. Even our thoughts will become *capitalist* thoughts!

And our despair?, W. wondered aloud. Is that what's left to us? Is that what remains of the good and the true? Is it in truly experiencing our despair that the path to our salvation lies?

Despair! W. took our audience through the twists and turns of *The Sickness Unto Death*. Of *The Concept of Anxiety*. He took them through crucial sections of Marx's *Capital*.

He conjured up a *bearded Kierkegaard* for our audience. A *melancholy Marx*!

And then W. gave me the floor. The room, abuzz with excitement during W.'s half of the presentation, fell silent. And I, too, was silent. The sound of construction from outside. The beep of a reversing vehicle.

Starting slowly, quietly, I began to extemporise on what I called the *time of stupor*, the *time of drifting*. I spoke about Tarkovsky's *Stalker*, about Tarr's *Damnation*. I spoke about *untensed time*, about *time out of phase*, about *temporal puddles* and *temporal ox-bow lakes*...

I spoke about Manchester as *rust-zone*, as *sleeper*. I spoke about the past and the rotting of the past. I spoke of those parts of the city that were cut off from time. I spoke of the *unregenerated* and the *unredeemed*. I spoke of the Sabbath, of the interregnum, of the great holy pause...

I spoke of *attenuated* despair, of grief stretched thin. I spoke of diffuse melancholia, and of the disorders of the vague. I spoke of the fear of the everyday — of cop show repeats on daytime TV, of *Columbo* and *Magnum P.I.* I spoke of stale beer and gingerbread men.

I spoke of falling to the level of the everyday. Of letting yourself fall. I spoke of watching the end credits of *Neighbours* not once, but *twice* a day. I spoke of what Perec called the *infra-ordinary*, and Blanchot, the *infinite wearing away*. I spoke of peripheries without centre, and of suburbs which never reach the city.

I spoke of nightbuses and eternal rain. I spoke of five hundred different kinds of boredom. I spoke of the wisdom of the long-term sick and the unemployed. I spoke of kebab wrappers blowing in the wind.

I spoke of empty hours and empty days. I spoke of wave-froth on the deep body of the sea. I spoke of misty thoughts yet to coalesce. I spoke of hazy skies and clouds of midges.

I spoke of being lost in time, buried in time. I spoke of time piling up like a great snowdrift. I spoke of time as an ache, as a wound, as a sigh. I spoke of space as a prayer, as a plea, as a poem.

I spoke of the nihilism of Joy Division. Of music which came from the other side of death. I spoke of rigor mortis and lockjaw. I spoke of the dancing chicken of Herzog's *Stroszek*.

I spoke of the anti-gravity of dub. I spoke of the Rasta-farians of Old Hulme. I spoke of *polytricks* and the *Babylon shitstem*. I spoke of the *exodus* and of *repatrination*. I quoted Prince Far-I: '*We moving outta Babylon/ One destination, ina Ithiopia... Ithiopia, the tyrants are falling/ Ithiopia, Britain the great is falling...*'

W. was moved, he says. I was moved. Our audience broke out into spontaneous applause. He'd thought my prophetic days had gone, W. says. He'd thought my oracle had shut up shop...

Almost all of them were working class, the Essex postgraduates, W. says. That's what must be understood. Working class, and with only instinct driving them to Essex.

All they had was a vague sense that life had gone wrong, somehow, W. says. That life had taken a wrong turn. That what had happened here in this country was, in its entirety, a *wrong turn*.

Some of the Essex postgraduates, it is true, had a kind of *folk-memory* of working class radicalism, of Nye Bevan and Henry Hunt, and, beyond them, of the Chartists and the Diggers. But most did not. Most had only an instinct, half-awake, half-alive, that there was something wrong, and not merely with them. Most had only the sense that theirs was not merely a personal problem, that their chronic depression, their chronic fatigue, their simply not fitting in, were not merely personal failures, personal foibles, matters of idiosyncrasy or maladjustment.

In fact, *there was nothing wrong with them at all*: wasn't that what the postgraduates discovered at Essex? Nothing wrong with them, and everything wrong with the world, especially Britain: wasn't that their first lesson at the University of Essex? Wasn't that put up on an overhead in their first lecture: *There's nothing wrong with you, and everything wrong with the world, especially Britain?*

Deprogramming: that's what the University of Essex provided. *Deconditioning*. It was like emerging from a cult, arriving at Essex, W. says. They needed exit counselling, the new postgraduates. They needed to be *deindoctrinated!*

W. thinks of those who didn't make it to Essex. Those who never got there, who had no idea of what waited for them there. Those who didn't even apply, and had no thought of applying. Those who applied nowhere, and would never think of making an application in their lives.

All those lost British Weils!, W. says. All those lost British Kierkegaards! There may even be a lost British *Rosenzweig*, sitting paralysed in Doncaster, W. says. And lost British Socrateses, who, like the original, will never write a line, but who will never meet their Plato. W. sees in his mind's eye a lost Diogenes, locked up in Strangeways for public indecency.

A lost Spinoza, W. says, working in *Specsavers* in Stevenage; a lost Descartes, company accountant in Earley; a lost Kant, working in Customer Services in Chipping Norton; a lost Buber, regional manager for a mobile phone company in Chalfont-St-Peter...

What might they have been had they passed through Essex! What might have happened had they been washed up on Essex's shore!

The train southwest.

He's been officially reprimanded for his teaching, W. says, reading his emails on his laptop. Making his students watch *Damnation* over and over again has no relevance to badminton ethics, he's been told. And the students don't want to hear any more Jandek, W. says. Actually, *he* doesn't want to hear any more Jandek. *He* can't bear it.

His sports science students lack a sense of the *eschaton*, W. says. They have no idea of the end times. How can he make them understand that there is no hope?

He misses the old days, W. says, when his philosophy students had to be *forcibly restrained* from throwing themselves from lecture hall windows. He misses the *honest despair* of philosophy seminars, W. says, when he and his students would speak of *thwarted lives* and *strangled chances*.

Philosophy *should* destroy you, W. says. Philosophy *should* break you to pieces. This is why Kierkegaard is so important. It's what Kierkegaard understands more than anyone else!

'*Since I was a child, I have lived under the sway of a prodigious melancholy. . .*', W. reads from his notebook. Ah, what can we understand of the *melancholy* of Kierkegaard — of his despair and its attendant suffering, of which he said, '*I was never free even for a day*'? What, of the '*premature aging*' of the Danish philosopher, which, he said, was caused by his melancholy? What, of his isolation, to which, he said, his melancholy condemned him — 'For me there was no comfort or help to be looked for in others'?

Kierkegaard saw his melancholy as a kind of *election*, W. says. As a kind of *calling*. For it was only loneliness and misery that revealed to him what matters most. Wasn't he to write, in the last period of his authorship, that *suffering was the sanctifying mark of God*? Kierkegaard thought that to accept suffering was the chance to *invert* its meaning, to regard it as an honour, as a source of pride. For isn't our suffering the analogue of Christ's on the cross? Isn't it an echo of the abasement of the apostles, who lived in poverty and lowliness? And doesn't it recall God's own suffering, when He sees what His church has become? '*There is truly a fellowship of suffering with God*', Kierkegaard writes. '*A pact of tears, which is intrinsically very beautiful*'.

But what happens when the pact is broken?, W. wonders. What, when suffering is no longer, as it was for Kierkegaard, a sign of God's love? W. reads me a quotation from Cesare Pavese's diary:

Suffering is by no means a privilege, a sign of nobility, a reminder of God. Suffering is a fierce, bestial thing, commonplace, uncalled for, natural as air. It is intangible; no one can grasp it or fight against it; it dwells in time — is the same thing as time; if it comes in fits and starts, that is only so as to leave the sufferer more defenceless during the moments that follow, those long moments when one relives the last bout of torture and waits for the next.

He's going to publish his essay on Cohen and Rosenzweig, W. says. His essay on the *mathematical* messiah. It's time to publish! Time for the thought-harvest! Time for the doors of the great archive to open, and for his essay to be ceremonially placed in the stacks!

What will the legacy of his essay be?, W. wonders. Fifty years from now, what will his essay have been? Will it have turned the world of Cohen, Rosenzweig and messianism scholarship *on its head*? Will it have given the world a new Cohen, a new Rosenzweig, and a new sense of messianism? Will it have *transformed the scholarly field*? Will it have become an *obligatory point of reference* for the scholars who came after it? Will W.'s name have appeared in a million footnotes, a billion bibliographies?

Will essays *for* and *against* W.'s interpretation of Cohen, Rosenzweig and messianism have been presented at colloquia and conferences? Will special editions of journals have been dedicated to his thought on Cohen, Rosenzweig and messianism, with W. having replied in turn to his scholarly respondents?

Will doctoral students have been unable to write theses discussing Cohen, Rosenzweig and messianism without referring to W.'s Cohen, W.'s Rosenzweig and W.'s messianism? Will a sense of the paradigm-busting significance of W.'s Cohen, W.'s Rosenzweig and W.'s messianism have passed into the popular imagination, into the pages of broadsheets and TV documentaries?

Will the scholars of Oxford have whispered of W.'s Cohen, W.'s Rosenzweig and W.'s messianism as they crossed college quadrangles ('Mathematical messianism! Of course! Why didn't we see it — Mathematics is the *key* to messianism!'; 'By Jove, what brilliance!')? Will the governing bodies of Cambridge have wondered whether to offer W. a Chair in philosophy ('The blighter! So he's finally done it...'; 'What a marvel! Dash it all, if I only had half his intelligence...')?

Will W. have received offers of American lecture tours and plenary talks? Will fellow scholars have stood on their chairs and cried, 'hurrah!', throwing their mortar boards in the air when they heard him speak? Will a ticker-tape parade have been held in his hometown, with W. being driven along waving to cheering crowds?

He feels light, W. says; the burden of his essay has been lifted from his shoulders. But he has a sense of purposelessness, of casting about. What will his next project be? Where next will he direct his academic labours?

His *Gottbuch*, his Book of God — might it be time for that?, W. wonders. His *Gottesbuch* — *Gott* is in the genitive, W. says, correcting himself. Is it really time?

Only at a certain point in your life can you begin such a project, W. says. Only once you have ripened. Is he ready yet?, W. wonders. Is it time to begin?

W.'s bored of his God researches on Wikipedia. — 'The train's no place for serious philosphy', he says.

A moment later. — 'Did you know that there are many different kinds of intelligence?', W. says. 'Wikipedia lists at least ten'. He's going to contribute an article of his own, he says. On the many different kinds of *stupidity*. After all, it'd be criminal not to share his findings with the world. Not everyone gets to observe a real live idiot at first hand.

One. *Linguistic* stupidity. My stammering, W. says. My stuttering. I can't *speak*. And I can't read!, W. says. Haven't I said that the sentences in the Krasznahorkai books which W. lends me are too long to follow? Didn't I say that *The Melancholy of Resistance* offers too little for the reader? And that *War and War* is too *boring*? — 'Boring!', W. exploded. 'Life is boring! Literature is not a celebrity magazine!' And then, 'Literature *should* be boring!'

Two. *Logical-mathematical* stupidity. I'm the last person to whom he would turn for assistance in his mathematical studies, W. says. How many times has he tried to explain to me the significance of the infinitesimal in the work of Rosenzweig and Cohen? How many times has he *drawn the graphs*?

Three. *Bodily-kinesthetic* stupidity. I'm not what he'd call a *graceful* man, W. says. How much have I spilt from our pint glasses, as I carry them from the bar? How many beer-trays have I dropped? It's my great flat feet, W. knows that. Didn't I have to wear special shoes as a child? He imagines a smaller version of me flapping along like a duck.

Four. *Interpersonal* stupidity. I've no sensitivity to other people's moods, W. says. To *his* moods, for one thing! How many times have I hurt his feelings?, W. says. How many times have I turned on him? It's always the way, after the first two days of drinking: I *turn*. I become nasty. It's very upsetting, W. says.

Five. *Intrapersonal* stupidity. This has to do with introspective and self-reflective capacities, W. says. With what Kierkegaard calls *inwardness*. He can imagine what I see when I look inward, W. says. There, where you're supposed to find the soul: only the expanse of the desert and the wind blowing. There, where you're supposed to find the centres of will and deliberation: only a surging ocean, filled with kraken. There, where you're supposed to find the seat of the intellect: only torn clouds, racing over the moon...

Six. *Naturalistic* stupidity. I've no feeling for nature, W. says, but then nor has he. In fact, he has a Jewish suspicion of nature ('It's unredeemed!'), and of the cult of the natural. But animals trust him. Robins would alight on the handle of his spade as he dug in his garden, if he had a spade or a garden. Squirrels would pick nuts from his outheld palm with their tiny paws...

You can tell a lot by what animals think of you, W. says. Animals watch me warily, he's noticed. — 'What's the ape man going to do?' Even plants seem worried, twisting towards W. for help.

Seven. *Moral* stupidity. I speak of myself in the *middle* voice, he's noticed that, W. says. In a voice that is neither active nor passive and that has neither a subject nor an object. It's to avoid all sense of responsibility!, W. says. All sense of blame! I would never say, *I've ruined W.'s life*, W. says. *There was ruination in W.'s life*, I'd tell him. I would never say, *I've soiled myself. There's been a faecal emergency*, I'd tell him.

Eight. *Existential* stupidity. Why are we here? What's it all for? Why is there something rather than nothing? Questions I've never asked myself, W. knows that. Questions he asks himself constantly! Why does Lars exist?: isn't that his first question?, W. says. Why is there Lars rather than nothing?

Nine. *Sartorial* stupidity. What's behind my Our-Man-from-Havana-after-twenty-years-on-the-beer look? What's behind my *footwear*? A thinker should dress for thought, W. says. A philosopher should be judged on his tops and his tails. He's lucky, because Sal dresses him, W. says.

Ten. *Religious* stupidity. I have no sense of God, W. says. No sense of monotheism! Oh, I have religious enthusiasms, W. grants that. Religious *Schwärmerei*. Sometimes, W. has felt moved to attribute a religious dimension to my despair over my life. To my warehouse years! To my years of unemployment and underemployment! But I've always fallen short of the idea of God, W. says. The idea of *messianism*. My Hinduism limits me, W. says. It's quite obvious.

Eleven. *Painting-and-decorating* stupidity. Why did I paint my living room pink?, W. wonders. What was going through my mind? Oh, he knows my answer: It was to bring out the red tones of the woodwork — of the built-in cupboards, with their louvre doors, I told him. But pink!, W. says. *Salmon* pink! He shakes his head. Of course, the pink is turning brown now, in big patches, W. says. It's turning green, too, and grey. Parts of the wall are spongy to touch. Parts of it seem to be becoming *hairy*. My posters of Louis Wain's cats do nothing to cover it up.

Twelve. *Romantic* stupidity. W. imagines my courtship display, spreading the peacock's tail of my idiocies. He imagines my great mating cry, like a wounded bull, W. says. But there will be no mating cry, and no courtship, he knows that. The word 'love' is completely meaningless to me.

Thirteen. *Culinary* stupidity. The discount sandwich is the opposite of food!, W. says. The desecration of food! A man cannot live on stale gingerbread men and *Kwik-Save* beer alone, W. says. Though I've tried to.

Fourteen. *Stupidity* stupidity. The stupid are invariably stupid about *being stupid*, W. says. They have no idea of their own stupidity! Others laugh at the idiot and he laughs along. Everyone's laughing!, he thinks to himself. What fun! The stupid person doesn't really *suffer* his stupidity, W. says. He leaves others to do that for him.

Passing through Exeter. Not too far to Plymouth.

How long is it since I wrote to our friend in Taiwan (W.'s friend in Taiwan)?, W. asks me. W. hasn't written to him in ages — years, he says. If you don't contact a friend in five years, then he's no longer a friend, that's W.'s principle. And to lose our friend in Taiwan (W.'s friend in Taiwan) would be a terrible thing.

Ah, how can he forget the sight of him, when we met him at the station? His weightlifter's vest... his Rupert the Bear scarf... Our hearts lifted! Our speaker had arrived, and all the way from Taiwan!

And what did we do with him? Where did we take him? W. shakes his head. To *the worst Chinese restaurant in Newcastle*. It was the only place open, I'd said. It's actually pretty good, I'd said. Our friend (W.'s friend) had travelled halfway round the world, crossed whole continents, and we took him to *the worst Chinese restaurant in Newcastle*.

It was my fault, W. says. My *Oriental food* enthusiasm. My *dim sum* enthusiasm. Surely a better restaurant was open in Newcastle in the mid-afternoon! Surely we could have found somewhere else to eat!

Our friend (W.'s friend) had travelled all the way from Taipei, Taiwan, a centre of great Chinese-style food, to Newcastle, which is in no way renowned for Chinese-style food,

W. says. Our friend (W.'s friend) had come the greatest distance possible, just to give a talk at my university, and we took him to a restaurant that would undoubtedly poison him and send him home in a body bag!

W. warned me, he remembers. What did he whisper to me on the way to Chinatown? *We mustn't poison our friend from Taiwan* (his friend from Taiwan)! But how could he have known?, W. says. How could he have known the hole into which I was leading him? *The Oriental Buffet*, W. says. All you can eat for £5, he says, shaking his head. *The worst Chinese restaurant in Newcastle.*

Our friend (W.'s friend) looked ill as we sipped our jasmine tea. *I* looked ill. W. *felt* ill, and that was *before* we began to eat. We hadn't even seen the menu! Hospitality is a great art, W. says. It's the art of arts. And here we were, as hosts, desecrating hospitality, spitting at it.

Still, he put a brave face on it, our friend from Taiwan (his friend from Taiwan), W. says. He took the reins of the conversation, as he always does. He was grace itself, as he always is. He tried to cover up the horror he must have felt at the dim sum, as it came glistening to our table. He didn't retch as he nibbled on chicken feet. The potstickers didn't seem to horrify him. He endured the steam buns and the spare ribs in hoisin sauce. And didn't he even finish off his mango pudding?

He survived the afternoon. *We* survived it! And when we met up later that evening, we were determined to take our friend from Taiwan (W.'s friend from Taiwan) for *a night out in Newcastle.*

There was a kind of *distractedness* to him, our friend from Taiwan (W.'s friend from Taiwan), W. says. A *vagueness*, as though he wasn't quite in tune with the world, wasn't quite in focus. His outline seemed blurred, his replies hesitant, W. says — didn't we notice that? When we asked him our questions, and we had many questions, there were long silences, great pauses and interregnums. And he replied, most often: *I don't know*. Because he didn't know, and he knew that he didn't know. He rested in non-knowing.

Ah, how far away we must have seemed to him, our friend from Taiwan (W.'s friend from Taiwan), with our inanities!, W. says. With our chatter! But he confided in us, W. says. He spoke of the *loneliness of thought*. He said that he'd been out too far, out too long...

He could only guess at the inner states of our friend from Taiwan (W.'s friend from Taiwan), W. says. He'd been out among the farthest stars, W. was sure of that. Out to the edge of the known universe, among the quasars...

Our friend from Taiwan (W.'s friend from Taiwan) had roamed anti-stars and anti-galaxies, W. says. He'd wandered out among the anti-electrons and the anti-baryons. He'd met the anti-Lars (a towering genius), and the anti-W. (very much in the shadow of his friend). He'd wandered to the end of time, and his thought was at one with the end of things: that was clear from his pauses and silences, from the gaps between his words. Between his sentences!

And when we took him out to the nightclubs of Newcastle, our friend from Taiwan (W.'s friend from Taiwan) seemed touched that we would think to look after him, W. says. He seemed genuinely moved when we showed him our *primal scene* dance.

We drank to his health. He drank to ours. We drank to his thought! He smiled at us. And when we took him to the airport the next morning, he embraced us both, looking each of us in the eye. — 'Pengyou', he said. 'Friend'.

As *friends of thought*: that's how we'll be judged, W. says. As friends of those made solitary by thought.

We've sought to assist thought and its thinkers. Sought to lighten the solitude of thinking. We've written consolatory emails (W. more often than me). We've praised and encouraged (again, W. more than me). We've even *discovered* thinkers, picking them out from the crowd (W., not me).

We're the encouragers of thought! Thought's enthusiasts! What thinker, in our midst, have we failed to cheer on?

Weren't we there, at our friend from Taiwan (W.'s friend from Taiwan)'s presentation, in the front row with our notebooks, furiously writing? He spoke, and we wrote. And after, knowing the audience's reaction could not fail to disappoint him, could not fail to leave our friend from Taiwan (W.'s friend from Taiwan) feeling yet more isolated, yet more alone, we all but bore him upon our shoulders, cheering. We all but deafened him with our cries.

What did he mean by this point, or that one?, we asked him. Stupid as we are, our interest flattered him. We were like a dry run, in our idiocy, for an encounter with a fellow thinker, an ally of thought, in conversation with whom our friend from Taiwan (W.'s friend from Taiwan) could rise to his true vocation.

And what would we do, if, when in company with our friend from Taiwan (W.'s friend from Taiwan), another thinker came along? What, if a conversation *between thinkers* truly began, if idea met with idea, like eagles rising into the air? We wouldn't get out our notebooks, W. made me promise that. I wouldn't take out my camera, my infernal camera, W. made me promise that, too. And we wouldn't chatter; we wouldn't say a thing: W. doesn't have to tell me that.

W.'s house, Plymouth. A pit stop for supplies, and to pick up books.

Why do I always take my trousers off in his living room?, W. wonders. On one level, the answer is obvious: I am growing too fat for them; their waistband cuts uncomfortably into my swollen belly. But then I never take my trousers off elsewhere, W. has noticed. Only in his house, with him and Sal. Only in his front room, whether the shutters are open or closed.

Once, when a friend of theirs called round unexpectedly, I leaped up, frantically looking for my trousers. Too late! — 'Lars always takes his trousers off when he visits', W. had to explain. I feel some sense of shame, at least, W. says. He didn't think I did, but there it was: shame over my trouserlessness. My *public* trouserlessness.

But why am I not ashamed of anything else?, W. wonders. My ignorance, for example. My laziness. He thought he'd taught me, W. says. He thought I'd learnt something. But somewhere inside, I'm still an ape on the savannah. Somewhere, I'm still sitting back on my haunches and looking out over the expanse.

Food was plentiful back then, on the savannah, wasn't it?, W. says. Life was easy. I wasn't an alpha male, of course, but nor was I an omega one. So long as I refrained from threatening my fellow apes, from baring my teeth as apes will, I was not threatened in my turn.

But something was missing on the savannah, wasn't it?, W. says. Something marked me out from my fellow apes. Was that why I learned to walk upright and wear shoes? Was that why I learned not to holler and whoop? But I never gave up my *ape dreams*, W. says. I never forgot to long for those great bunches of bananas and clear pools of the jungle.

He can tell I'm still an ape, W. says. It's the way I hold my pen — the way my hand curls in towards my chest. And there's that distant look I get, W. says, as though I long only to tear open my shirt and whoop. But my *apish spontaneity* is long gone, W. says. I am no better off than my miserable comrades in the zoo, my poor eyes burning from monitor glare, and my clumsy fingers missing the keys.

The books I try to read! The thinkers I try to imitate! At times, he thinks he'd put a stop to it, if he didn't see something of himself in my efforts, W. says. If he didn't feel as though he, too, were part ape.

Sometimes, W. wonders whether he is my captor — whether he was the one who trapped me on the plains. But it wasn't his fault! I was placed in his care, W. says. Didn't he tenderly look after me? Didn't he suckle me as gently as an orphaned fawn?

Once, I was an ape with no idea of trousers. And now, thanks to him? A half-ape, for whom trousers are a tyranny.

He, too, was once looked after, W. says, lovingly tended by the older Essex postgraduates. He knew comparatively little when he first arrived at Essex, W. says. He had only a sense that he had to think *against* Britain. As though thought were a way for him to struggle back to Canada. As though he might reach a kind of *Canada of thought*.

And years later, when he saw the new postgraduates arrive? When he saw them arriving from the four corners of the country? He was tender with them, W. says — fatherly, perhaps even *motherly*, never laughing when they mispronounced the words *hyperbole* and *synecdoche*, or when they said the last syllables of Derrida to rhyme with *breeder*, or when they said Del-*ooze* when they meant Del-*erze*?

He understood when the new postgraduates wept into their pillows, W. says. He stroked their hair during their night-sweats and bad dreams. He knew why they ground their teeth at night, why their jaws ached, why their eyes were dull: for wasn't he, too, British? Hadn't he, too, sought to escape his country at the University of Essex?

Late night, W.'s living room. An empty bottle of Plymouth Gin before us.

W. remembers the *guest speakers* of Essex University. Envoys from Old Europe. Thinkers who had been taught by the gods of Old Europe — by Heidegger and Merleau-Ponty — and who spoke of the gods of Old Europe. Thinkers, who were friends and contemporaries of Deleuze, of Foucault, and who spoke of the world of Deleuze and Foucault. Thinker-experts, who'd spent their whole lives in the archives, or studying in seclusion with the works of a Master. Thinker-militants, who'd hung out with Debord and Vaneigem, and who could pass on stories of Debord and Vaneigem.

Literary scholars, who read in twenty-seven languages. Philosopher-scientists with advanced degrees in astrophysics and molecular biology. Thinker-mathematicians, fascinated by *dissipative structures* and *complex systems*. Thinkers of *irreversibility* and *indeterminism*, of *strange loops* and *paralogic*...

Neurophenomenological thinkers, W. says. Neo-Spinozist thinkers. Neo-Leibnizians. Nominalists and anti-nominalists. Mathematical thinkers and *poetical* thinkers.

Thinkers who'd had distinct *phases* in their thought. ('In my early writings, I was convinced that...'; 'Later on,

I concluded that...'; 'For a long time, it was my impression that...') Thinkers whose work was the subject of conferences and roundtables.

Thinkers who hated other thinkers ('Don't mention Deleuze to him!'). Thinkers who'd broken with old friends over intellectual matters. Over *political* matters. Thinkers *at war*, for whom philosophical enmity had become *personal* enmity, had become name-calling, and hair-pulling.

Thinkers who'd shot away half their faces in despair, W. says. Thinkers with deep scars across their wrists. Thinkers who *wept* as they spoke. Thinkers whose pauses were longer than their talks. Thinkers in breakdown, their lives careening. Thinkers who spoke frankly about the misery of their existence. Thinkers who told of why they couldn't think, why thought was impossible, why the end had come: their end and the end of the world.

Wild thinkers. *Drunk* thinkers. *High* thinkers, nostrils flared, pupils tiny, staying up for whole weeks at a time. Thinkers with missing teeth. With missing *eyes*. Thinkers with missing fingers, and with great clumps of their hair torn out. Thinkers with terrible rashes around their mouths.

Sick thinkers, walking with two sticks, W. says. *Coughing* thinkers, who could hardly get out a word. Thinkers who spoke too quietly to be heard. Thinkers who spoke *too loudly*, half-deafening the front row. Thinker-declaimers, thinker-prophets who might as well have set themselves on fire in the seminar room.

Exiled thinkers, forced out of their home countries for *crimes of thought*. *Lost* thinkers, left over from vanished intellectual movements. *Bereaved* thinkers, in mourning for dead thinker-partners. *Betrayed* thinkers, who spoke of backstabbings and purgings, of auto-critiques and revolutionary punishment.

Thinkers with neck-kerchiefs, W. says. Thinkers with cravats. Thinkers with Hawaiian shirts (Jean-Luc Nancy, after a trip to the USA). Thinkers in plus-fours (Jean-Luc Marion, heading up to Cambridge to try and impress the dons). *Thin* thinkers, in roll-neck sweaters, with sharp cheekbones and shaved heads. *Tubby* thinkers, epicureans full of joy, with great, jolly faces and thick folds of fat at the back of their necks. *Worker*-thinkers, with thick, flat fingers and spadelike hands, who'd laboured alongside others in the fields and the mines. *Serene* thinkers, half godly, looking into eternity with widely-spaced eyes.

Laughing thinkers, who laughed because they could think, because they were free to think. Thinkers who'd escaped from imprisonment and war. *Saintly* thinkers, of unimaginable integrity, of absolute purity. *Nomadic* thinkers, who, like swifts, never touched down, moving only from conference to conference as invited speakers. *Traveller* thinkers, who had forsaken the lecture circuit for private voyages through jungles and deserts. *Ascetic* thinkers, who spoke of great solitudes, great retreats. Thinkers who had *seen* things, *lived* things that were greater than they were.

Thinkers who knew what it meant to live. Thinkers who served life. Thinkers who thought in order to live, and to be alive. Thinkers who spoke of the *ecstasy of thinking* after their talks, in the student bar. Thinkers who spoke of the *beatitude of thought*, tears glittering in their eyes. Thinkers who said, *the only thing that mattered was to think*.

Bearded thinkers, with great bushy beards like Marx's, or tidy, trim beards like Lenin's, or goatees like Trotsky's, or — very rare — *neckbeards* like William Empson's. Nona-genarian thinkers. *Centerian* thinkers! And thinker-youths, no more than twenty years old, mere pups, with minds like steel traps.

Thinkers who'd been imprisoned for thinking, W. says. Thinkers who'd been half-crucified for *blasphemies of thought*. Thinkers whose tongues had been ripped from their throats. *Mute* thinkers, whose papers were read for them. Thinkers whose voices were hoarse from screaming. Thinkers who *refused to think*, out of shame, and refused to read their own paper, out of modesty.

Humanist thinkers, dripping with pathos, W. says. *Anti*-humanist thinkers, siding with viruses, siding with plagues, waiting for the demise of 'man'. Thinker-fanatics, full of hatreds and ecstasies. — 'Your kind', W. says.

The Essex postgraduates met them all, W. says. All the thinkers of Old Europe.

We're hungover. The light hurts our eyes. 'Is there hope for us, any hope?', W. wonders on the bus out from Plymouth to Dartmoor.

'*The destiny of this life is that it be brought to the uttermost of life-disgust*': that's Kierkegaard, W. says, reading from his notebook. Have we reached that point?, W. wonders. *The uttermost of life-disgust*: how hungover would we have to be, to be brought to that? How much would we have to had drunk?

It's the kind of day you might come across a corpse, we agree, as we walk out on Dartmoor. It's the kind of day someone might come across *our* corpses.

'God's watching us', W. says. 'Can you see?' But I can see only brown bog and the overcast sky.

W. tells me about the wild Dartmoor ponies, left to wander on the moor. And he tells me about the Beast of Dartmoor, which attacks the ponies, leaving their entrails steaming in the morning sun.

W. points to the abandoned longhouses of the high moor, more than a thousand years old. One day they'll be occupied again, W. says. One day, there will be people who come up to the moor, looking for shelter. Exiles, like us. Freed slaves with long hair and guitars, as gentle as deer...

The rain clears. The open sky. — 'It's come to this', W. says. 'The final reckoning'. And then, 'You can't hide on Dartmoor. You can't keep secrets'. And then, 'It's just us and our God. The God of twats'.

They'll find us lying prone, with our eyes pecked out. They'll find our bodies half-eaten by the Beast of Dartmoor. Yes, that will be our judgement.

We've gone missing, W. says. Well, *he* has. They should send out search parties. There should be men with loudhailers calling his name. He's lost on the moor, W. says — on *my* moor. He's lost in the wilderness, W. says — in *my* wilderness.

Melancholy, melancholy: sometimes W. feels half-drowned by its waves. And don't I feel something of it, too, as we wander through the heather?

The melancholic cannot leave behind what he mourns, Kierkegaard says. He comes to identify with his loss, to think of himself as nothing other than his loss. His life, his very existence, is indistinguishable from a kind of *tomb*.

The melancholic tends not to know what he's lost, Kierkegaard says. He has only a vague sense of deprivation, a general sense that something has gone missing. God: should that be our name for it?, W. asks. God: is that the name for *our* loss?, W. wonders.

Sometimes he wants to curse God, W. says, as Kierkegaard's father did as a young man, herding his sheep on a Jutland heath. But he doesn't believe in God, W. says. So how can he curse the *non-existence* of God? How can he shake his fist at the sky?

At other times, he wants only to *localise* his loss, W. says. And he doesn't need to look further than the idiot beside him in his cagoule. '*It must be the idiot's fault!*', W. thinks to himself. He wants to shake me, to grab me by the lapels and bellow, 'It's all your fault!' Because it *is* my fault, he's sure of it.

But what if he's wrong? What if I'm only a *scapegoat* for his problems? The Hebrews used to send a goat into the wilderness, which was supposed to carry with it the sins of the people, W. says. And is that why W. has brought me up to the moor, he wonders: to send *me* into the wilderness, carrying all *his* sins away?

'*There goes my loss*', W. would say, watching me disappear into the distance. '*There go my sins*'. And he'd walk more lightly on his way back to the bus stop. He'd sing to himself. The clouds would part...

But what if grief remained with him, and as heavily as before? What if despair never lifted itself from his shoulders? Horror: now he'd be alone with the storm-cloud of his grief. Now he wouldn't have an *idiot in a cagoule* to blame for his melancholy.

Am I his Abraham or his Isaac?, W.'s never been sure. Will I take him to be sacrificed on Mount Moriah, or will he take me? God's told him nothing, W. says. He's listened in vain for the command to lead me to the mountain.

But what has God told me? If I know anything, I'm keeping quiet. In fact, I've been especially quiet lately, and W.'s caught me looking off into the distance, as if seeking out a local equivalent of the Biblical mountain.

But perhaps the sacrifice has already occurred. Haven't I *ruined W.'s reputation*? Haven't I *publically humiliated him* again and again? God never stayed my hand, W. says. God never told me to sacrifice something else in W.'s place. He's an Isaac whom God did not deign to save, W. says.

W. thinks of Job on his ash pile. Job, afflicted with boils, his possessions destroyed, his children killed, sitting scraping his skin with shards of broken pottery. Job, who, when his wife told him to curse God, reproached her: '*Shall we receive good from God and not receive evil?*'

Never did Job question divine providence. Never, even though he cursed the day he was born.

And what of him, W.? How many times has he thought to curse my presence in his life? How many times has he shaken his fist at the sky, and cried, 'Why me God? Why me?' But no answer has ever come. The whirlwind hasn't spoken.

Is he still being tested? Am I his trial, his burden? Elihu counsels Job that he should expect no explanation for his travails from God. God is not to be questioned. Then is it only when W. stops shaking his fist at the sky, when W. stops asking why, that the whirlwind might speak?

Dartmoor is all that's left of the commons, W. says. Of the land that used to be of all and for all; of the treasury of the earth, where everyone could glean and forage. He speaks of how landowners enclosed the good land of the valleys, of the plains, fencing off the common land of the villages and towns. Only rough pasture was left, W. says. Only the wastes and barren lands, where people could live '*out of sight, or out of slavery*'...

The gypsies came to Dartmoor, W. says. Looking for pasture. Looking for vistas! And Devon Robin Hoods, look- ing for a hideout from which to launch their raids. Escaped peasants, fleeing peonage. And there were would-be *revolu- tionaries* too: *Ranters*, dreaming that the earth would be held in common again, that the land would belong to all, like the sunshine and the breezes; *Levellers*, working and eating together, joining hands with Christ to lift up creation from bondage; *heretics*, who prayed that the enmity of all lands would cease, and that none would dare seek dominion over the others, nor desire more of the earth than another...

And now? Today? W. hopes that some new outsiders will come from the valleys and the plains. That some new Moses will lead the new slaves from their Egypt to the high moor.

W. wants to press the *cosmic rewind button*, he says. He wants to rewind the history of Dartmoor, past the clearing of the woods and forests and the building of longhouses. He wants to rewind to a time before agriculture — to a time when the earth was as yet untroubled by the hoe, unwounded by the ploughshare. He wants to rewind to a time before any sense of rights and ownership. To a time before granaries and food surpluses! To a time before work, and war, and priest-kings and hierarchies!

W. wants to reach the point when groups of hunter-gatherers first crossed the landbridge to Britain, dogs at their heels, following herds of red deer...

The path leads upward, to where the river Dart is supposed to have its source. This is where the water they use in Plymouth Gin comes from, W. says. It's the peat that gives it its special softness. And the way it's filtered through granite.

W. passes me his hipflask. We've brought our gin back to its wellspring! To its Eden! We've completed the circle. We drink to the Dart, and to the rain that feeds the Dart. We drink to the clouds, and to the seawater that evaporates to make the clouds. We drink to the sea and to the rivers that feed the sea.

We drink to our digestive systems. Our gin-processing systems! And we fantasise, as we drink, about a *thinker of the moors*, a thinker lost on the moor like King Lear and twice as mad as him. About a thinker whose madness *is* his thought, W. says mystically.

Is that really a rainbow?, W. says. The sign of the covenant, W. says. The sign of God's promise at Sinai. The promise that bound together the Hebrew tribes escaping from Egypt, W. says. Into a people. Into a *kingdom of priests*. A *holy nation*.

At the beginning of the march, when they had just set out, the Hebrews' commitment to God was great, W. says. They were leaving Egypt, leaving their captivity. Who could be more willing? Who, ready to sacrifice more?

Then the murmurings of discontent began, W. says. Then, the frustrations about blisters and the desert heat. The Pharaoh at least *fed* his slaves!, the Hebrews murmured. He at least gave them some modicum of shelter!

What the Hebrews didn't understand was that the desert was a test, W. says. That the people had been delivered from their captivity to undergo suffering. That the *pedagogy of the desert* was necessary, if they were to purge themselves of the humiliations of their servitude.

But when Moses descended from Sinai, with the tablets of the Law, glowing in his hands?, W. says. There was no more backsliding! No more nostalgia! Forward to the Promised Land! Forward to Canaan! The Hebrews carried the Law in the Tabernacle, W. says. They knew what should be done.

Some rabbis have said that many covenants were made at Sinai, not just one, W. says. 603,550 covenants were made, these rabbis have said — a covenant between each of the Hebrews and God. But other rabbis have said that covenants were made between each Hebrew and the totality of his neighbours; that there was a total of 36,427,260 covenants — 603,550 multiplied by 603,550, each person pledging himself in service to the others. It was not enough for each to act justly, these rabbis have said. Each had to see his neighbour act justly, taking on his neighbour's sins as his own. Each was responsible for his neighbour, for his neighbour's shortcomings. It was only thus that the holy nation could become an *ethical exemplar* to the rest of humankind, W. says. It was only thus that it could be as God said, that this people *'shall be unto me a kingdom of priests'*.

A kingdom of priests: that's what W. dreams of being part of: a holy nation. But we're not much of a nation, W. and I. Not much of a kingdom! If only we could find others to walk with us! If only there were others who would come with us to the promised land! But our friends are scattered and at war with the world. God knows, they have their own problems.

And what of us, who leap like mountain goats over tiny tributaries of the river Dart? I am responsible for him, W. says. But what is much worse is that *he* is responsible for *me*, for all the sins I have committed. And that means that I am the obstacle to W.'s crossing into the promised land. That I am the desert across which he has been doomed to wander.

'Everything lies in the hands of God except the fear of God':

that's what is written in the Talmud, W. says. But when you have no fear of God, as I have not? When the word *God*, means nothing at all, as it means nothing at all to me? What is he going to do with me?, W. wonders. How is he going to teach me the meaning of *sin*? Because you have to have some sense of *shame* in order to understand sin. And when shame is entirely lacking...?

At least Moses had his Levites, his faithful!, W. says. At least he had a vanguard who understood the real meaning of Canaan! Ah, what W. would do with a Levite or two, with friends who might think alongside him! With a *phalanx* of Levites, standing shoulder to shoulder, their shields locked together and their spears poking out. Each Levite holding the other's place in the line of battle. Each sustaining the other's courage...

Of course, the Promised Land is only a name for the *messianic epoch*, W. says, when each person, seeing to the salvation of his neighbours, becomes the Messiah. When each lives in accordance with the Law, W. says. When each plays with the Law, as one child with another.

And until then?, W. says. Even the lushest countryside is a desert. Even the heathery bogs of Dartmoor are but an infinite expanse of sand.

Why didn't he join them, the former Essex postgraduates, who fled Britain?, W. wonders. Why did he stay behind?

There's a story by Kafka — a parable really, W. says. The Master demands that his servant saddle up his horse. 'Where are you riding to, Master?', the servant asks. — 'I don't know. Away-From-Here, that's my destination'.

Away-From-Here: that's where the Essex postgraduates went. Away-From-Britain. That's where he should have gone, W. says: Away-From-Britain. He should have stayed overseas after his studies.

Why did he come crawling back? What secret fatality led him home? Why was he chained to Britain as a dog to its vomit? Was it some inadequacy? Some sense that he didn't belong among the cafés and cobbled streets? Was it British inadequacy? British stupidity? A British inability to take himself seriously as a thinker?

Away-From-Here... But he'll never get away, will he?, W. says. There's Canada, of course, his Canadian dream. But the Canadian universities don't even reply to his job applications. They don't even send him rejection letters...

He's been *left behind*, W. says. He and some of the other former Essex postgraduates, who found academic jobs instead of leaving Britain. They compromised, he says, they who had been shown that *life is elsewhere*, and that one should try to struggle into that elsewhere; that life flared into its fullness somewhere else, in another place; that life moved in Old Europe like fire in fire, like weather on the sun...

Life was elsewhere. Life *is* elsewhere, that much is clear to him, W. says.

A chance, a promise. That's what they were given, the Essex postgraduates. Life was elsewhere... They lived in the wrong age, and in the wrong country. They were men and women out of time and out of place.

Their ideas weren't British ideas, or at least not *current* British ideas, W. says. Their ideas weren't *commercial* ideas, ideas that belong to the new reality. Ah, in another country, they thought back then, things would be completely different.

Wouldn't they have been taken by the arm and treated with great politeness and interest in *Mediterranean* countries — in religious or recently religious countries — where you can still discuss Cohen and Rosenzweig over olives and chorizo? Wouldn't they have found allies and admirers in the countries of *Eastern Europe* — in political or recently political countries — where you can still discuss Marx over your weissbiers, where Weil and Kierkegaard are on everyone's minds?

Of course, they all study philosophy at school, in Old Europe, the Essex postgraduates knew that. Everyone knows a little something about philosophy. Everyone has something philosophical to say. It's in their blood. In the air! It's in the *aether* of Old Europe, the Essex postgraduates said to one another. It's in the cafés and wine cellars. It's in the city squares and riverside parks. And can't you see it shining out in the faces of children?

Old Europe, Old Europe. But its day was passing, the Essex postgraduates knew that. And so the promise of *their* day was passing, they who never really knew Old Europe. Their philosophy would die unnoticed: how could it be otherwise? The ideas of Old Europe would not take root here.

They would have to fly off elsewhere, the Essex postgraduates, as dandelion seeds of thought. They would have to take root in South America, perhaps — in Argentina, which is supposed to be a very thoughtful country, a real *thinking country*; in Columbia, which has philosophy departments like great castles; in Uruguay, which probably already harboured the thinker-friends who would take the next great leap of thought.

Or they would have to reach fertile ground in vast China, vast India, or in overcrowded Japan. Somewhere, someplace else, they would have to find the *countries of thought*. Somewhere beyond Europe, itself no longer fertile soil for the ideas of its thinkers...

Ah, its time had come, Old Europe. Its time was already overdue. Old Europe had already outlived itself, was already posthumous. But didn't it dream nonetheless? Didn't it send its dreams back from the other side of death? Were *they* Old Europe's dreams, the Essex postgraduates?, W. wonders. Were they the way Old Europe dreamed of coming once more to itself, now and in Essex?

Now and in Essex, now and in Essex. W. has always had a waking dream that our country might become the next *country of philosophy*. He's always dreamt — and he knows it's ridiculous — that something might begin in our Britain: that a day might come, that the chance of a day might come. That the sunrays from old Europe, from the sun-touched countries of the south, might burst through our northern clouds. That a heavenly fire might illuminate our ancient landscapes and break across our upturned faces...

And on that day, that bright impossible day, our tears would flow, W. says. Our hearts would melt, our knees buckle. We would fall into the arms of thought. Thought would be as easy as falling. We'd speak to each other at last. We'd hear each other speak — at last, at last!

The train to Edinburgh.

    W. reads to me from his notebook:

A rabbi, a real cabbalist, once said that in order to es-
tablish the reign of peace it is not necessary to destroy
everything nor to begin a completely new world. It
is sufficient to displace this cup or this brush or this
stone just a little, and thereby everything.

Imagine it! Two plastic cups of Plymouth Gin might usher in
the *reign of peace*, W. says.

    There's no gin, so we settle for cans of Stella from the
trolley. To the sea!, we toast, banging our cans together.

He doesn't really *know* the North Sea, W. says. He doesn't
really *feel* it. What lies across the water, for instance? He
doesn't even know that... Denmark, I tell him. Travel east,
and we'd reach Jutland, and the port of Esbjerg. Ah, the
land of the Vikings!, W. says. — 'Your people, pillaging and
marauding...'

    Of course, I've always maintained that the Vikings have
been misunderstood by history, W. says. They were a melancholy people, first and foremost, I've told him. A people of
tungsind, of heavy-souledness, I've insisted.

The Vikings knew their time had passed, I've told W.
They knew that their Ragnarok was due; that a new religion was coming that would sweep the old one away. It
was because Christianity was coming to their northlands that
they sailed to Lindesfarne and smashed the Abbey, I've said
to W. And it was a sense of their own posthumousness that
drove them to pillage and maraud their way across Christian
Europe.

And wasn't it the same heavy-souledness which drove
them to the New World, to settle in Newfoundland? Wasn't
it Viking heavy-souledness that led them southwards, down
the coast of present-day North America, all the way to what
became Mexico? They wanted to escape, I've told W. To
escape themselves! To leave themselves behind! That's why
they founded Viking settlements along the edge of East Africa,
and in pockets of India, where blue-eyed, heavy-souled natives
claim ancestry from lost Danish colonies.

We must be gentle with our Edinburgh friend (W.'s Edinburgh friend), W. says. He is the most delicate of men, as thinkers are often delicate. The most fragile. His poor health... his withered arm... his spasms and tics...

But as he shows us around Edinburgh, our Edinburgh friend (W.'s Edinburgh friend) seems anything but fragile.

The New Town was going to be built in the form of a Union Jack, our Edinburgh friend (W.'s Edinburgh friend) tells us, and we marvel. Imagine that! He tells us the story behind the Act of Union, which saw Scotland united with England in order that its rich elite might gain access to the market of the English colonies. '*We were bought and sold for English gold*', says our Edinburgh friend (W.'s Edinburgh friend), quoting Rabbie Burns. And on the day the treaty was signed, the bells of St Giles Cathedral rang out *Why Should I Be Sad On My Wedding Day*...

How well-informed our Edinburgh friend (W.'s Edinburgh friend) is! How much he knows! He's so much *cleverer* than us, we agree. Of course he's cleverer than us! He's more *studious* than we are — of course he is! He's more of a *scholar* — of course!, of course!

For how long has our Edinburgh friend (W.'s Edinburgh friend) been working on his Bergson book? For how long, having studied advanced mathematics in order to explore mathematical themes in Bergson, and having mastered *mathematical German*, in order to read the latest German papers on Bergson and mathematics?

And he's more *interdisciplinary* than we are, our Edinburgh friend (W.'s Edinburgh friend). Hasn't he patiently consulted his colleagues in science about the scientific aspects of his study of Bergson?

And he's more *cutting edge* than we are; his work is of more contemporary relevance. For, his Bergson study is by no means a merely historical study, a matter of the *history of ideas*. Our Edinburgh friend (W.'s Edinburgh friend) is writing *a study of Bergson for our times*, showing how Bergson's thought might be understood to be abreast of our times, if not ahead of them.

And our Edinburgh friend (W.'s Edinburgh friend) is more *generous* than we are, more thoughtful. Didn't he take us out last night for the finest of whiskies? Didn't he baulk at the idea that we would pay for our rounds of whiskey — didn't he, indeed, *insist* that he would pay for every round, and even choose the whiskies for us?

And hadn't he already bought the finest of wines for us, knowing we were coming, with our taste for wine? And the finest of cheeses, knowing of our enthusiasm for cheese? And hadn't he readied himself with concerned questions about our lives and the *trivialities* of our lives, things that should concern no one, least of all a thinker such as he?

In the end, it was a terrible crime that a thinker like him, our Edinburgh friend (W.'s Edinburgh friend), should fill his head with such trivialities, instead of filling it with more materials relevant to his Bergson project. To his *unfinished* Bergson project, for it is unfinished, and has remained so for several years.

And how did we repay him? What did we do after we drank all his wine and ate all his cheese? What, after he listened so patiently to our woes? We buttoned his carefully folded shirts over our teeshirts; we rolled on his carefully hung trousers over our shorts and got under his neat, folded bedclothes. — 'We're thinkers!', we cried, imitating his Edinburgh burr. 'We're men of ideas!'

'What are you doing?', said our Edinburgh friend (W.'s Edinburgh friend), aghast. — 'We're going to write a book on Bergson', we said, in our approximation of his accent. 'We're going to write a study of Bergson for our times!' We were completely giddy. — 'What are you doing?', our Edinburgh friend (W.'s Edinburgh friend) asked again and again. Didn't we hear in his voice something of the *betrayed trust* of a solitary thinker? Didn't we sense the solitariness that we had invaded? That we had *defiled*?

We were in his sanctum. He'd shown us his chamber of thought, and the implements of his thinking. We'd seen his bookshelves, for God's sake, which he revealed with the tender shyness of a virgin...

We'd seen his bookmarked volumes of Husserliana. We'd seen his complete editions of Reid and Hume, and his broken-spined Greg Batesons. We'd seen his threadbare *Fractal Geometry of Nature*, his Prigogine and Stengler. And we'd seen books on *self-organising systems* and *catastrophe theory*, on *non-linear modelling* and *complex criticality*.

He'd taken us (well, W. at least) to be fellow thinkers. He'd spoken to us (to W.) as peers, as thought-compatriots. He'd thought we (W.) were non-trivial men, *serious* men, *men of ideas* like him. He'd thought we (W.) were *Hyperboreans*, men of altitude and vision...

Oh God, how puerile we are!, W. says. How *delirious*! Why did we let our inanity sweep us away? Why do we destroy whole friendships (W.'s friendships) with our foolishness?

There was a time when W. thought there was a kind of *freedom* in our lightness. That buffoonery was a kind of liberation, a release from false gravity. At least we're not *pompous* men: isn't that what he said to himself?

But he knows now that there is no end to inanity, that it's like sliding on ice, W. says. That there's no friction, nothing to stop you … and that we've long since slid past each one of our friends (each one of W.'s friends).

The people we've disappointed! The friends we've estranged! W.'s full of remorse, he says. Full of guilt! — 'Do you remember Nashville?', he says. 'Do you remember what we did to our Canadian hosts?' We bickered in front of them, I remember. We argued. — 'We did more than that', W. says. 'Do you remember the night we sang about cocks?' Ah, *cock song night*; of course.

Once again, we went too far, W. says. Our host had a guitar, he recalls. We were to sing together, to share the songs of our countries, our childhoods. We were to sing, as Canadians like to sing after dinner. For a Canadian, W. explained to me, it's only natural to sing after dinner. To sing, and to listen to others sing, and perhaps to learn new songs, and perhaps to teach songs to others.

But what did *we* sing?, W. says. What songs did *we* send floating up into the night? — 'Songs about cocks', W. says. 'Our great cock songs'. We drowned the Canadians out in our excitement. We drowned them out in our hilarity.

We let ourselves down again, W. says. *He* let himself down. Wasn't he supposed to be the sensible one in our party? Didn't he feel himself *personally responsible* for our behaviour?

W. compares us to our Edinburgh friend (his Edinburgh friend): he gives, we take; he has ideas, we plagiarise; he engages with the real world, with contemporary ideas, contemporary science, while our engagement with the world is entirely mediated by books we half understand.

Our friend (W.'s friend) tries to change the world; we are utterly parasitical on people who try to change the world. He makes people feel funny and intelligent; we make people feel depressed and demotivated. Every day, for our Edinburgh friend (W.'s Edinburgh friend), something new might occur. Every day, for us, only confirms that nothing new will ever have occurred.

W. blames me, he says. I've infected him. I've given him some kind of disease. Some kind of cancer of the brain, W. says. Parts of his brain have turned to mush, he's sure of it. If you cracked open his skull, it'd be full of cottage-cheese-like mush. I've *curdled his brain*, W. says. That's why he's become so inane. That's why he's losing his faculties one by one.

The faculty of reason — that went long ago. The faculty of politeness — oh, it's going, he can feel it, W. says. The faculty of acumen — long gone. The faculty of non-stupidity — turned into mush. The faculty of wit — curdled. And now all that's left of him is the *non-faculty* of inanity, and the *anti-faculty* of stupidity.

Edinburgh morning: it's a song in our hearts, this city. Coming out from our hotel, we feel a great upsurge of tenderness. Opposite, spread before us, the Old Town rises up in layers. We tremble with love — don't we feel *lighter* here in Scotland? Isn't the air fresher, keener? And we have the whole day before us! We have time, the whole day, like an empty expanse.

Scotland always makes us forget, we agree. Scotland always gives us the gift of oblivion. Have we really forgotten the disaster of last night? Have we really put it behind us, the desecration of our friendship with our Edinburgh friend (W.'s Edinburgh friend)? We have. Selective forgetting: this is the secret, W. says. Voluntary amnesia. It's what allows us to go on.

The train to Dundee.

W. looks through my notebook. Notes on Robert Walser's confinement. Names and dates. Ah, very interesting, W. says. Didn't Walser *volunteer* to be taken into Herisau sanatorium? Didn't he want to go there for the *peace and quiet*? He'd had enough of the world. Enough of the writer's life. No more poverty! No more garret rooms! No more rejection letters! And no more writing!, W. says. No more of the *will* to write!

> *At the sanatorium I have the quiet that I need. Noise is for the young. It seems suitable for me to fade away as inconspicuously as possible.*

> *One lies like a felled tree, and needs no limbs to stir about. Desires all fall asleep, like children exhausted from their play.*

To fade away; to lie like a felled tree; to be blown around the world like a leaf. What Zen master has ever wanted to achieve more?

Walser wanted to disappear, W. says. He wanted to dissolve into the everyday like some kind of *mystic of the ordinary*. It's what *I've* wanted, he knows that, W. says: it's what I've sought in my years of unemployment. Haven't I wanted to become a *man without qualities*?, W. says. Haven't I said I wanted the everyday to smooth away my distinctness, like a river does to a pebble?

It's what gives me a strange kind of *wisdom*, W. says. A strange kind of *religiosity*! Sometimes, he's even thought of me as a kind of *saint*, W. says. As a holy man of the banal; a hermit of the empty hours.

Haven't I been a kind of suburban Saint Anthony: a man who ventured into the deepest of suburban deserts? Haven't I wrestled with the most banal of demons, and passed obscure trials which have left others drunk or dead?

What vacancies I have known! What boredoms! What diffuse despairs! The everyday still clings to me like bits of shell to a hatching chick, W. says. It's why, in the end, he has a kind of respect for me. For isn't the everyday the contemporary equivalent of the Biblical desert?

The next page in my notebook. Notes on Hölderlin's confinement. *Pallaksch*, W. reads. — 'What does that mean?' That was the word Hölderlin repeated to himself in the thirty years he spent mad, I tell W. Pallaksch!, he sang out, as he played his piano madly. Pallaksch!, he cried up to the night, when he couldn't sleep for mania.

Pallaksch!: that should be my word, too, W. says. My word for what roars in everything I have written or tried to say. He hears it in my stuttering, my stammering. In the 'hellos!' that I boom out to near-strangers. And isn't pallaksch! what I'm trying to say when I use the middle voice? *There was a dampening. There was an infestation of rats. There was a proliferation of Japanese knot-weed.* Pallaksch! Pallaksch!

Faecal emergencies come, one after another, W. says. Toilet bowls are spattered. The gods, blind and deaf and mad, are screaming. The sky is darkening. The desert is growing. He can smell sulphur, W. says. He can see black wings... Pallaksch! Pallaksch! Pallaksch!

Kierkegaard *foresaw us*, W. says, flicking through his note-book. He knew we were coming. Why else would he write so many pages on the dangers of *religious enthusiasm*, of *drunken religiosity* and of *religious phantasmagoria?*

'*The despair of possibility is a lack of necessity*', Kierke-gaard says. Ah, Kierkegaard knew us well, W. says. *The fan-tastic, the unlimited*: this is what Kierkegaard most abhors. The dangers of an imagination unlimited by anything con-crete.

Hasn't our inclination always been towards the vague, the amorphous? Haven't we always tended towards the grandest of vistas, the most epic of pronouncements?

We've taken drunkenness and ecstasy for religion, W. says, when really religion is sobriety and steadfastness. We've taken unbridled speculation and cosmic pathos for philoso-phy, W. says, when really philosophy is rigour and argu-ment...

W. tells me of the legend among Essex postgraduates of the *last thinker*, the thinker of the end of times, the thinker of the alpha and omega of thought.

Of course, you'll never be able to tell who the last thinker is, W. says. He'll look like anyone else. At least that's how W. sees it: the last thinker himself won't understand his significance, like a god who's forgotten he's a god. Like an amnesiac Messiah.

Perhaps it's the last thinker W. seeks, when he attends early morning conference sessions. Perhaps that's what he looks for in the thinkers he invites to stay with him in his home. W.'s waiting, in his own way, he says. At any moment, his guest will be revealed in his glory. At any moment, it will be the last thinker, the Messiah of thought, who sits across from him.

Is *Lars* the last thinker?, W. sometimes catches himself wondering, as he walks beside me on the street. Is *Lars* the thinker of the end of times?, he muses sometimes, watching me eat my chips, tomato ketchup staining my jumper. Probably not, W. thinks.

From the greatest stupidity, the greatest thought, W. sometimes says to himself. Will the last thinker — the thinker who will wrap it all up, the Messiah of thought — be distinguishable from a perfect idiot? The last thinker, the perfect idiot: they're versions of the same figure, in W.'s imagination, he says. They're the same person, viewed in different ways.

Is idiocy the path to thought, or thought the path to idiocy? Is perfect thought the goal, or perfect idiocy? W.'s not sure of the answer.

W. would be impressed by my studies in the Bible — you say studies *in* the Bible, not *of* the Bible, W. says — if I weren't so drawn to the apocrypha. And not just the official apocrypha, but the *apocryphal* apocrypha.

I have a taste for the spurious, W. says, for dubious angelology and extravagant miracles. I like the Gnostic gospels in which Jesus kills dragons with death-rays from his eyes. I like the vignettes of the beasts of the desert kneeling before the divine child, and of the palm-trees bowing down so the holy family can pick their fruit.

And haven't I spoken to him of hoping to find a *caped* Jesus, a *flying* Jesus, a *gospel of the superman*? I must take my Biblical studies more seriously, W. says.

My idiocy draws me closer to God than he is, W, says, and all the more because I profess no belief in God whatsoever. What does God mean to me? Nothing, says W., but on the other hand — everything, *because* it means nothing.

God means too much to him, that's his trouble, W. says. The *idea* of God. But I have no idea of God. I have no ideas, and this is what saves me.

Leuchars. Invergowrie. The farther north we go, W. says, the more civilised it becomes. The more socialist! Scotland is the refuge of socialism, W. says. Think of Red Clydeside! Think of the Radical War!

Scotland is closer to the social democracies of Scandinavia, that's what does it, W. says. Scotland breathes Scandinavian air. He's always been impressed by Scandinavian social democracy, W. says. High public spending! The redistribution of wealth! Universal health care! Early retirement! These are the signs of a real civilisation, W. says.

The only future for Scotland is to dissolve the Union, W. says. To dissolve it, and then set itself adrift like the stone raft of Saramago's novel, heading north, only north...

The frozen north: that's where the purest kind of politics might be found, W. says. It's only with other people that you can withstand the Arctic winter, he says. Only huddled together for warmth — and what is politics but a huddling together for warmth?

W. speaks of the far north of Scandinavia, and the far north of Canada; of white expanses and trackless forests; of swirling snow and frost flowers spreading on the window. He speaks of the warm hearths of the far north; of oil lamps hanging with crystal prisms. He speaks of Canadian laughter in the glittering light. Of Canadian merriment during the endless winters!

Canadians leave their doors unlocked in the frozen north, W. says. They leave their hearts open! The law of northern hospitality means that you have to take anyone in who knocks at the door. '*The stranger who dwells among you shall be to you as a home-born, and thou shalt love him as thyself*': that's what is written on Canadian walls.

You can know nothing of human society until you stamp the snow from your boots in a Canadian hallway, W. says. Until you've clinked glasses with your Canadian hosts. The storm gathers outside; but you sit warm by the fire. The snow lies deep; but you drink and sing with your Canadian hosts...

Dundee Arts Café, after our presentation. 'The elephant in the room was your stupidity', W. says. And then, 'Actually, *you* were the elephant in the room. My God, you're fatter than ever'.

Conference Sunday. W.'s drinking extra coffee to ease his melancholy. Soon we'll leave our friends (W.'s friends). Soon we'll scatter again, and W. will be alone with his guilt. Why can't he help his friends more? Why can't he be a better person? These are the questions he constantly asks himself.

Ah, was it only two days ago that W. embraced his friends, some of his old Essex compadres, with tears in his eyes? There was much hugging and weeping, W. says. They broke into song, the old songs of Essex, Wivenhoe river-shanties... They toasted their teachers, and the guest speakers of Essex... They celebrated the memory of the brilliance of their contemporaries, and of their own youthful brilliance...

The stories they exchanged! The camaraderie! Ah, but what could I understand of any of that?, W. says. Was I ever part of a cohort? Was I ever part of a group of friends who shared above all the desire to *push one another to greatness*?

I was only ever on the run from the suburbs, W. says, running first to Kafka and then to Kierkegaard, running first to literature and then to philosophy. And I'm still running, only I've long since run into administration and bureaucracy.

Still running, although I'm fat and breathless now, which makes it even more grotesque.

Why don't I ask questions anymore?, W. wonders. Why don't I intervene, after the presentations?

He remembers the questions I used to ask, W. says. After every presentation! My voice, booming out! My voice, resounding beneath the vaulted ceilings! For a time — a long time — no conference presentation was complete without one of my booming questions. There'd be no conference discussion in which I didn't have my say.

W. remembers the questions I asked in the warmest and stuffiest of lecture rooms. He remembers my interventions in the final hour of a long day of presentations. In the final *minute!* I cut through the fog like a samurai sword. I broke through the torpor. It was marvellous, W. says. — 'Your lucidity! Your far-sightedness!'

Then what happened?, W. wonders. How did I end up so sullen and uncommunicative? I became silent, he says. Surly. I sat with folded arms, and took no notes.

W. remembers the notes I used to take. Pages and pages of them! With diagrams! In different colours! He remembers the array of pencils and pens I used to line up beside my notepad. He remembers my underlinings and exclamation marks. He remembers me writing *No!*, or *Yes!* beside my notes in capital letters.

What happened?, W. wonders. Do I still have questions in my head? Do questions still burn somewhere inside me? There's no sign of it, W. says. I sit, W. says. I slouch. I look vacant, as if post-lobotomy. I let it all wash over me — presentation after presentation, speaker after speaker.

It means nothing to me now, does it?, W. says. All thought, all philosophy. I am a mollusc on the shore, W. says. I am a pebble on the beach, simple and impermeable. I am lost in the shingle, as the waves break over me.

He thinks we *depressed* our audience, W. says. We moved them, it's true, but in the wrong way. Sometimes that can happen. We tried to bring them through despair to hope, we agree, but we think we left most of them in despair. — 'It's the morose look on your face', W. says. 'It's your hangdog expression'.

We spoke briefly of the history of despair, taking in Aristotle's theories, and those of Avicenna and the Desert Fathers. We spoke of Burton's great *Anatomy of Melancholy*, and of Benjamin on left-wing melancholy.

And then we spoke of the *despair of capitalism*, our speciality. We spoke of the despair of the *un*employed and the *under*employed. We spoke of the despair of the exploited and the disenfranchised. We spoke of the despair of sham happiness and fake friendships. We spoke of empty smiles and hollow hearts. We spoke of our despair at the *representation of life*, when real life is elsewhere.

We spoke of *turbo*-capitalism and *nano*-capitalism, and of marketing niches no bigger than the individual. We spoke of the hyper-differentiation of target markets, and of adverts designed for you and you alone. We spoke of the destruction of even the *chance* of a labour movement, and even the *chance* of a politics. We spoke of broken hopes, of the great *dividing and conquering*.

W. spoke movingly of his years of whoring for work as a would-be lecturer, and then I spoke movingly (W.: 'less movingly') of *my* years of whoring for work as a would-be lecturer. W. spoke of nearly being sacked for political agitation, and I spoke of being sacked over and over again in my years as a temporary contractor in the Thames Valley.

W. spoke of the poor of Plymouth, and I of the poor of Newcastle. W. spoke of the derelict houses on his street, and I, of the human derelicts who wander my city.

We spoke of the *broken lives* of capitalism, of sweat-shop workers and slum-dwellers... We spoke of open sewers and shit-clogged barrios. We spoke of kidney farms and faecal dust. We spoke of the denizens of chemical dumps and of the slopes of volcanoes, of the dwellers in railway sidings and oil refineries. We spoke of cities of straw and scrap-wood...

And, opening a kind of parentheses, W. spoke of my flat. — 'My God, you should see it!', W. said to our audience. 'It's disgusting!'

We spoke of the false infinity of financial speculation, and the false future of the futures market. We spoke of fool's gold. We spoke of the shit at the end of the rainbow. We spoke of the great golden calf of Mammon.

And we spoke of the future, of whole peoples on the move, and of the great barriers raised against them. We spoke of the ever-spreading desert, and the hardening of the earth. We spoke of the silent spring and of the harvest of dust.

With God, everything is possible; that's Kierkegaard, we said, with the fervour of true believers. To embrace God is to embrace possibility in the midst of necessity, the infinite in the midst of finitude, we said. It is to embrace *freedom*.

Reality — the necessity of the real, the reality of

capitalism — is only a temporary thickening of possibility, its hardening, we said. From the side of *actuality*, of *capitalist actuality*, possibility seems like nothing at all. But from the side of *possibility*, of *faith*, it is capitalism that is nothing, nothing but a scab to be scratched from the skin of life.

We spoke of Kierkegaard's account of possibility, which transforms despair into joy. Through the possible, '*I experience everything more perfectly, more accurately, more thoroughly*', we said, quoting Kierkegaard, '*even if it is only the sight of grouse bursting upwards into the sky of a Jutland heath*'.

And that's what we must learn to see, we told our Dundee audience: grouse bursting upwards from the heath of our unbelief.

On a bench behind *Little Chef*, staring out at the Firth of Tay.

Journey's end. The tour's over. 'Do you think you've learnt anything?', W. asks. No. He hasn't either, he says. Actually, he thinks he's forgotten things. He thinks his learning is decaying, W. says. His thought is rotting. As a result of our tour, the level of European culture has sunk a little bit lower.

Did we really think we could escape the end of philosophy?, W. wonders. Did we really think we could make a philosophy out of the end times, when the end times means: the end of philosophy?

Plan A's collapsed, W. says, and there is no Plan B. There's only fantasy after the collapse of Plan A... But what kind of fantasy? — 'What are your dreams, fat boy? A cream cake as large as your head? A swimming pool full of corn nuts?'

He dreams of *politics*, despite everything, W. says. He dreams of the *act* that will redeem our lives. We've failed as thinkers, he says. He knows that. But as *activists*?

What became of them, the Essex Postgraduates?, W. wonders. What, of the would-be thinkers touched by heavenly fire? Oh, not the ones who found jobs, not the *state* philosophers and *state* political theorists; but the others — the *wild* philosophers and *wild* political theorists, the thinkers driven out, and those who drove themselves out.

What happened to them, those known thereafter only by the stray signals they sent back? What, as they loosened themselves from old bonds, old friendships, and contact with them became intermittent?

Some disappeared completely. Where did they go?, W. wonders. Did they change their names? Did they go underground? Did they travel to the four corners of the earth in search of obscurity? Is that what they found in the mountains of Yaktusk: obscurity? Did they manage to disappear in the ice deserts of Antarctica? Did they lose themselves in the rebuilt Shanghai or in the favelas of Rio de Janerio? Did they hole up in the Aleutian islands to write a magnum opus?

Did they wander like Japanese poets through the stone forests of Yunnan, leaving traces of their passage in fragments of as yet unwritten philosophical masterpieces? Did they take to the steppes to think and write in secret, getting ready for their magnificent return? Did their heads seem to explode as they lay beneath shooting stars on Goa beaches, bombed out on ketamine? Did the pain seem to radiate out of them like light as they volunteered to be crucified in Pampanga?

Some devoted themselves to politics, W.'s sure of that, to militancy, to joining the Zapitistas, to signing up with the Naxalites in India. Still others became partisans, became insurgents, became foragers of the scrubland, nomads on the plains, ever on the move, ever watchful. Some deserted to head further into the wilderness, further into obscurity. Some were known only as *missing persons*, their relatives searching for them in third world jungles, their friends leaving tributes on Facebook pages.

Some became ill, mentally ill, W.'s sure of that, too. They wanted derangement, to derange themselves. They wanted insanity, seeking it by every means: by drugs, to be sure, but also by ascetic rigour. '*We must become what we are*', they said to themselves. '*Each one of us is his own illness*', they said to themselves. And so they sought to *intensify* their illnesses, to drive them deeper, and then to enter wholly into them as into a secret fissure.

Some sought solitude, silence, wanting not to express themselves, but to have nothing to say. Some gave up thought for art, for anti-art, making sculptures in the wild, sculptures out of the snow and air, for no one to see. Some wrote great poems, then burned them, watching the pages crispen and catch fire. Some wrote great philosophical treatises and tossed the pages into the wind.

Some sought to lay waste to their lives, to throw them away. Some sought to sacrifice themselves to nothing in particular, wanting only to squander what had been given to them. Some drank themselves into oblivion. Some smoked themselves into vacancy. Some blew out their brains on hallucinogens.

Some wanted to become just like anyone else; no: more

like anyone else than anyone else, as anonymous as possible, as buried in ordinary life as possible, taking the most mundane of jobs, leading the most mundane of lives.

Some, in W.'s mind, sought to think *without* thinking, to write *without* writing. What matters is to live this 'without', they said to themselves, very mysteriously. What matters is to live *outside* thought, *outside* writing...

Some gave in to bouts of despair, throwing themselves into rivers and oceans. Some gassed themselves in bedsits, some launched themselves through sixth-floor windows. Some reddened the snow with chunks of bloody brain and skull. Some broke their knuckles punching walls. Some pissed themselves in gutters, and shat themselves in holding cells. Some cut open their bellies and spilled their guts into the air.

Some took upon themselves all the miseries of the world: some cut their throat because they believed themselves responsible for them; some drove swords into their chest because of what they hadn't done to prevent them.

Some sought to side with the proletariat, earning no more than the proletariat, gleaning fruit and vegetables from market stalls, and clothes discarded in warehouse bins. Some sought to live alongside the proletariat, and the *lumpen*proletariat: the thieves and vagabonds. Some lived among those who have fallen beneath the proletariat: the displaced, the stateless, refugees who had escaped deportation.

Some half-drank themselves to death to live with the alcoholics. Some destroyed the bridge of their nose sniffing solvents, sniffing turps, to live among the solvent-sniffers and the turps-sniffers.

Some became recluses, shutting themselves up inside;

some became *hikkikomori*, living with their parents but not seeing them, subsisting on food left outside their bedroom doors. Some took holy vows and disappeared into monasteries. Some became self-flagellants and self-scourgers. Some joined cults; some started them. Some preached on the street about the end of the world. Some tried to *bring about* the end of the world, to call the end closer.

Some sold themselves as mercenaries, some as prostitutes. Some joined the FBI, others the Foreign Legion. Some sided with the rats and the cockroaches, and dreamed of being eaten alive by rats and cockroaches. Some wanted to be devoured from the inside out, and longed for biting termites to creep into their nostrils, to crawl into their ears. Some came to side with *viral* life, with bacteria and protozoa, and dreamed of a world without humans, without vertebrates, without any kind of higher life.

Some, tormented by thought and the demands of thought, sought to destroy their very capacity to think. Some sought to slice off their own thinking heads; some placed a bit to their skull and began to drill. Some drove pencils through their nostrils into their brain. Some shot themselves through one eye, and then another. Some asked — *begged* — for lobotomy. Some, for their brains to be sucked out of their skull. Some, to be left perpetually asleep, aging silently. Some, to be forced into a coma; some, to be battered into a state of imbecility.

The Firth. Light flashing across the waters.

Away-From-Here..., W. says, no louder than a whisper. To go out, and never come back... He quotes Burroughs:

'*It is necessary to travel, not to live*'. He quotes Gysin: '*We're here to go*'.

We're here to go: that's what the Essex postgraduates knew, even though it brought so many of them to destruction, W. says. That's what *he* knew, W. says, even though he didn't join their exodus. Even though he was a coward.

Should we make up for it now?, W. wonders. Should we head further north? Should we catch the train to Aberdeen, and then to Inverness? Should we take the ferry to the Shetland Islands? To northern Norway?

He knows we will never reach our Canaan, W. says. Canaan is for the young. But we could be the advance-scouts of Canaan. We could go to its brink, and report back.

He sees us, in his mind's eye, heading into the north, into the storms of the north, W. says. He sees us sailing across the cobalt seas, the aurora borealis flickering on our faces. He sees the days grow longer, the skies lighter, as the parallels converge. And one bright day, our team of huskies pulling us across the snow, we'd see the promised land shimmering in the distance. Is it a mirage of ice?, we'd wonder to ourselves. Is it an effect of glittering light? And as we'd come nearer, we'd see it for what it is: *Hyperborea*, the legendary land behind the north wind, which admits only the most youthful and proletarian of souls...

But what would happen in reality? They'd find our bodies just off Inverness, W. says. They'd dredge our bodies from the water. He sees the headlines: *Lecturers Drowned on Idiot Quest*.

His colleagues wear tracksuits to work, and have whistles around their necks, W. says on the phone. He can see them doing star-jumps outside his window. He finds it oddly hypnotic, he says. It soothes him when he looks up from his reading.

No one *laughs from the heart* in his university, he's noticed that, W. says. Not anymore. There's no joy in the corridors. Even the sports science students seem subdued, as they play lacrosse on the college greens.

And how is it at my university?, W. asks. But he knows the answer. — 'You're doomed — dooooomed!' And what am I going to do about it? I should think about a *dirty protest*, W. says. A *pre-emptive* dirty protest. — 'Go on. Strip down and smear the walls with your shit. That'll show them'.

'Are they're still building?', W. says. Always, I tell him. Night and day. They're starting a new excavation now, I tell W. The basements have been dug — very deeply, almost to the centre of the earth — and foundations laid, I tell him. The superstructures are going up — and the formwork, and anchors for hoists. They've dug great trenches for service pipes, in long rows, like burial pits...

W. hopes they'll dig deep enough to awaken the sleeping King Arthur. He hopes they'll stir the sleeping Frederick II, the sleeping Charlemagne. He hopes they'll stir the *last thinker*, who lies buried most deeply of all...

W. sends me the essay questions he's set his students.

1. *In Vino Veritas*. What have you learnt from drinking?

2. '*I am outside the truth; nothing human can take me there*' — Simone Weil. Do you consider yourself to be inside or outside the truth?

3. '*Salvation always comes from where nobody expects it, from the depraved, from the impossible*'. Explain, giving examples, what Rosenstock means by i) the depraved, and ii) the impossible. Do you agree with him?

4. '*Nobody can truly say of himself that he is filth*'. Is Wittgenstein right? Are *you* filth? Explain why/why not.

5. '*Our talk of justice is empty until the largest battleship has foundered on the forehead of a drowned man*'. What does Celan mean? Answer with reference to badminton ethics.

6. 'I think joy is a lack of understanding of the situation in which we find ourselves'. Is Tarkovsky right? What do you think he means by 'the situation in which we find ourselves'?

7. 'There are not only social problems. We have some ontological problems and now I think a whole pile of shit is coming from the cosmos'. Distinguish between what Tarr means by social shit, ontological shit and cosmological shit with reference to i) *Damnation*, and ii) your life.

8. 'There is no more university, only a game of ceremonies. Rectors, deans, lecturers, students, all move to cover over the void, a void that is covered over by the rules of dead time'. Do you agree with Blanchot? Discuss with reference to our college.

9. What is the significance of the dancing chicken in Herzog's *Stroszek*? Explore with reference to i) your life, ii) the cosmos.

10. 'Salvation will come, but only when we choose despair' — Kierkegaard. Have you chosen despair? Why/Why not?

Something terrible is going to happen, he knows it, W. says on the phone. He *feels* it. This morning, he found himself weeping without reason. He felt overwhelmed by an unaccountable sadness, by a melancholy that seemed to be without cause. — '*Why so downcast, my soul?*', he whispered to himself, quoting the Psalms. '*Why do you sigh within me?*'

Is this what Kierkegaard meant by anxiety?, W. wonders. But he's not anxious about himself, or about his relation to God, W. says. It's not his own existence which worries him, his own soul. Something's changed in the world, he's sure of it, W. says. Any minute now, and it will become clear to everyone. Soon, it will be there for all to discern.

W.'s reading Norman Cohn again. *The Pursuit of the Millennium*. How many times has he read this book?, W. wonders. How many times has he tried to scry the future in its crystal ball?

W. reads about the flaring of millennial hopes outside of the institutions of the church — about the processions of naked penitents crying to God for mercy. He reads about the flagellants — vagabonds, outlaws and criminals of all kinds — whipping themselves to atone not only for their own sins, but for the sins of the world. He reads about the *prophetae*, who discovered signs of the Millennium all around them — in raining frogs and stones and fish, in the lightning above the churches and graveyards, in solar eclipses and shooting stars — signs that the great Deliverer was about to appear.

Is *our* Deliverer about to appear?, W. wonders. Is *our* Millennium on its way?

Wars and rumours of wars between philosophy departments, and between colleagues in philosophy departments; stories of lecturers hating and betraying one another, and taking out grievances against once another; terrible falls in student recruitment, in National Student Survey rankings; terrible rises in student litigation, in student complaints made to the university authorities; the appearance of *false philosophers* in the media, deceiving many; the rise of the scoffers of philosophy, who spit upon philosophy; the proliferation of *introductory* books on philosophy, as opposed to *real* books of philosophy; the triumph of *applied* philosophy, of *applied* ethics, which is to say, *compromised* philosophy, the *opposite* of ethics: the signs of the end are everywhere, W. says.

Petitions are circulating about staff redundancies, about department closures. Petitions against capitalism in the university, against the private partners of the university.

Don't they realise that the petitions come too late?, W. says on the phone. That they ask for too little? We ask for too little! The university has to be *remade*, W. says. Turned *inside out*! We have to expose the university to everything it has tried to exclude. The working class, the unemployed... The street-drinkers, the vagrants...

W. recalls Deleuze's legendary seminars. Anyone could come to them! You could just wander in off the streets. People did! Deleuze would speak for hours, lost in a cloud of cigarette smoke. When the hubbub from the audience became too much, he'd pause to take questions from the floor — mad questions, vagrants' questions... Or he would simply pause, his tender eyes surveying his audience, half-amusedly, half-lovingly. And then he would begin again, as though he hadn't been interrupted. Deleuze had folded the outside into the university, W. says.

W. recalls the protesting students and lecturers of the May '68 Events in Paris. Lacan's daughter, giving out degree certificates to strangers on the bus... Foucault, charging the police with the crowd, batons bouncing off his head...

Derrida, equivocating as usual, wondering whether to act as usual. Badiou, doing *revolutionary maths*...

The university was in the streets!, W. says. They'd turned the university *inside out*!

The moment's come, W. says on the phone. They're closing the philosophy department at Middlesex.

W. imagines them like giant crabs, the destroyers of philosophy. As giant crabs with great metallic claws. But in the end, they'll only be managers. Manager-murderers, with profit-and-loss spreadsheets.

'It'll be our turn next', W. says. 'They're coming to get us'. The cursor, on someone's monitor, is already hovering over our names.

What will happen to the Middlesex researchers?, W. wonders. What will become of them? There are no jobs in philosophy — everyone knows that. No jobs in academia!

They'll be turned out into the world, W. says. Exposed to the four winds... How will they maintain the strength that is necessary for thinking? How will they sustain their self-belief? Their *commitment*?

They'll have their brilliance, that's true, W. says. Brilliance will still throb in their temples. They'll have their intellectual projects, half-finished as they are, it is true... But no one will understand their brilliance when they leave the university, W. says. No one will appreciate the importance of their work! And they, too, will begin to forget. They, too, will begin to lose a sense of their own brilliance, and of the importance of their work...

The shelterless thinker is a *vulnerable* thinker, W. says. It takes great strength to be a Maimon, a thinker-vagrant. Great courage to be a Chouchani, who was part of no institution.

W. reminds me of Robert Lenkiewicz, the Plymouth Rembrandt, who used to let vagrants live in his studio. There were about fifty of them at any one time, W. says, dossing down among the huge canvasses, most of them crazy, most of them disturbed, screaming and shouting through the night... Should W. take the new vagrants of philosophy into his study?, he wonders. Should he offer the vacant rooms of his house to the sacked philosophers of Middlesex?

W. knows that I'm incapable of feeling anything about Middlesex, and for our friends in Middlesex (his friends in Middlesex). I fear only for myself, for my own position.

Ah, what haven't I done to keep my job?, W. says. What won't I do? I'm craven, W. says. Cowardly.

I tell him about endless management meetings, and the constant process of review. I tell him about the continual rewriting of business plans and self-assessment documents, of writing reports about reports about reports...

W. imagines me in my meetings, a version of Shostakovich before the Politburo, a political prisoner, moving between stupid defiance and servile obedience.

How abject I must be! How pitiful!, W. says. — 'How many fingers am I holding up?', my interrogator will ask me. Fuck off!, I'll shout. And then, pitifully, How many do you want me to say there are? Yes, he can see me in his mind's eye, W. says: a gorilla in a suit, pleading for his life.

I would have been happiest in the period of show trials and autoconfessions, W. says. I would have liked nothing better than to have confessed to imaginary crimes — the greater, the better — signing every confession the police brought to me, and admitting my role in the greatest conspiracies. It would have given me a sense of importance, of epic grandeur. *I did it,* I would say. *I was the worst of all.*

It was me, it was all my fault: what have I ever wanted to say but that?

Why, in the end, do we mind so much about our departments being closed down?, W. wonders. Haven't we always thought we should be destroyed like rabid dogs?

Ah, but our punishers have no idea of our sins (of my sins), W. says. They don't understand our shortcomings (my shortcomings). It's their *indiscriminateness* we object to.

Haven't we always dreamt of receiving a great sentence and execution?, W. says. Haven't we always dreamt of a night swarming with vengeful angels, and of St Michael's fiery sword?

We're not afraid of being judged, W. says. We're not afraid of answering for our sins. But they'll murder us in the night, these new executioners. They'll kill us in ignorance, without realising why we *should* be killed, why we *deserve* it. We'll *go down*, but not in the name of anything in particular.

This is why we'll have to stand our ground, W. says. To save, not the ones we are, but the ones we could have been, those whose places we hold. To honour, not what we might have achieved, but what they might have achieved, had everything been different.

The desert is growing, W. says. I'm writing more, much more than he can follow, on my blog, my infernal blog. Posts about him. About us! It's remorseless. Thousands and thousands of words. Day after day.

Don't I know there's a war on — a *philosophical* war?, W. says. Why am I not marching to the philosophical front lines, like he is? Why am I not *doing my bit*?

His sports science students are complaining, W. says. They don't see the relevance of Sun Tzu and Clausewitz to *badminton ethics*. They don't understand why they're being made to study the guerrilla tactics of Mao Zedong in a module on *shot-put metaphysics*.

'*War has no constant dynamic*', W. quotes, '*just as water has no constant form*'. '*The skilful strategist defeats the enemy without doing battle*', he quotes. '*The enemy advances, we retreat*', he quotes. '*The enemy sets up camp, we harass. The enemy tires, we attack. The enemy retreats, we pursue*'.

If he can't make his sports science students into a *guerrilla army*, W. says, he can make them into beasts of burden instead. Hasn't he dreamt of saddling them up and *riding* them, placing bits between their teeth? *Philosophical* bits! The bits of Rosenstock! Of Rosenzweig! Hasn't he dreamt of kicking literary spurs into their sides? The spurs of Kafka! Of Krasznahorkai!

W. dreams of mounting his last postgraduate students on the backs of his sports science students. Of combining brain and brawn, like Master/Blaster in *Mad Max III*. Then, he and his army would take to the hills, W. says, and get ready to charge the college in a few months time.

There are turning points in our life, W. says. Conversions. Sometimes we're *called*, he says. Sometimes we're allowed to become better than we are. God knows, that's what we need.

What set of events would let us *come into our own?*, W. wonders. He sees us in his mind's eye, clearing the rubble after a great earthquake. He sees us with a band of monk-brothers, heading into the desert. He sees us nailed to crucifixes, martyrs to some great cause...

To disappear into a larger movement!: isn't that what he wants?, W. says. To be dissolved anonymously into some great work of goodness? He'll have to bring me with him, that's the problem, W. says. I'll be trotting alongside him, tugging at his habit, asking when we're going to stop for lunch.

The trick of politics is knowing when to act, according to Debord, W. says. You have to study the *logic of politics*. You have to learn lessons from it. And, sometimes, you have to set the rules yourself, and follow those rules through to the end.

We need a strategy!, W. says. We need tactics! We need to aim our blow, as Clausewitz puts it, on the centre of gravity of the whole war. And it *is* a war, W. says. Politics *is* war, at the end of times.

Political despair: that's what we should guard against, W. says. Political *defeatism*.

The danger is that we are in love with the *loss* of politics, W. says. That we are happy with it; that we *depend* on it. That we love Britain, even as we pretend to hate it. That we love *capitalism*, even as we rave against it.

There's always a danger of revelling in our woes, of taking refuge in them: that's what Kierkegaard warns us of, W. says. We need to *intensify* our despair, to despair over it, that's what Kierkegaard tells us, W. says. We must despair over our despair! We must *double* up our despair, set despair against despair, if we are ever to transform it into action!

The Essex postgraduates never succumbed to left-wing melancholy, W. says. They never thought that history was at an end, or that there could be no alternative to capitalism. Some of them, it is true, advocated a kind of *hyper*-capitalism, a *turbo*-capitalism, which would accelerate capitalism to its end. Some of them held out for a capitalism-gone-berserk, a *deranged* capitalism, which would destroy half the world as it destroyed itself. But the Essex postgraduates never lost faith in the *utter transformation of the world*, W. says. They never supposed that politics could be anything other than *all-enveloping*. They never thought that politics could mean anything but *a total revolutionary project...*

Tomorrow it was May: isn't that what the Essex postgraduates said to themselves? Tomorrow it will be May '68 again. Tomorrow the occupations will begin. Tomorrow, the general strike. Tomorrow they'll set cars on fire and barricade the streets. Tomorrow they'll heave up the paving stones...

All he knows is that it will be necessary for us to *go under*, W. says. That, whatever happens, it will be a younger generation that will begin anew...

No one will remember us (no one will remember *him*), W. says. No one will know what we tried to do (what *he* tried to do), W. says. No one will know what he had to put up with...

Just as Moses never entered the promised land, only seeing it from afar, so we will never enter the promised land of the new politics, W. says. Just as Marx and Engels didn't live long enough for the Russian revolution, so the new revolution will only come after we have disappeared from the scene.

W. dreams of Dartmoor as the Canaan of the British postgraduate. He imagines long-haired postgraduates reroofing the deserted longhouses with thatch, and resowing the moor with woodland. He imagines them spinning wool and curing hides in the sunshine. And he imagines the children of the postgraduates roaming the wild, following herds of red deer, as their ancestors did when they crossed the landbridge to our country. He imagines them constantly on the move, braving all weathers, owning no more than they can carry. And he imagines them *singing* as they wander, letting new songs echo in the forest glades. Songs of love and friendship... Songs of the open sky... Songs of the new world, of the new Stone Age.

'What songs would you sing, after the end of the world?', W. asks me. Cock songs, I tell him. He can see us now, W. says, singing out our great cock songs as the world ends around us.

The last thinker of Essex Postgraduate legend will come on the last day, which the Germans call the *youngest* day, W. says. He'll come in the last hour of the last day, wreathed in clouds; in the last *minute*, and lo!, every thinking eye shall see him. He'll come in the last *second* of the last minute, and all the enemies of thought will wail because of him.

And the last thinker will set down the book he carries with him, which is known as the Book of Life, W. says. And he'll unlock its seven seals, one by one, and stand back as, with each seal, a terrible vengeance is born.

When he opens the *first* seal? A *white* horse will go out, with a white rider, clothed in fire, and raze the universities of the southeast, W. says. And when he opens the *second* seal? A *red* horse will go out, with a red rider, clothed in blood, and raze the universities of the southwest. And the *third* seal? A *black* horse will ride out, with a black rider, cloaked in the night, and raze the universities of the northwest. And the *fourth* seal? A *pale* horse will ride out, with a pale rider, clothed in winding sheets, and raze the universities of the northeast.

And when he opens the *fifth* seal? Those expelled from their jobs, those sacked from righteous departments, will have white robes given unto them. Postgraduates who never finished their studies, who broke themselves against the texts of

Heidegger and Derrida and Deleuze: they too shall be robed in white. Undergraduate geniuses, brighter than a thousand suns, who never received funding for postgraduate study: they too shall wear robes of white. Thinkers who were kept *outside* the university, obscure Judes who lived their entire lives in employment precarity; thinkers of unimaginable integrity, unimaginable will, reading Leibniz in their lunchbreaks, reading Canguilhem on the commuter train: they too will be robed in white. Thinkers too *mad* to think; *institutionalised* thinkers; alcoholic thinkers lying ruined on park benches, who were never given a chance: they, too, will be lifted up and clothed in white.

And the *sixth* seal? There will come a great thought-quake, a shaking of books. The sun of thought will become as black as a sackcloth of ash, and the moon of thought as red as blood. And the false stars of thought — the careerists and pontificators; the popularisers and dumbers-down; the *depoliticisers* and *despiritualisers* — will fall unto earth. And the false heaven of thinking, full of endless publishers' series of introductory books: *Philosophy in 60 Minutes, Great Thinkers in an Afternoon, Locke in Your Lunchbreak, Maimonides in a Minute, Socrates in a Second,* will be rolled up like a scroll... And the enemies of thought — the resenters and the zealots, the pompous and the privileged, the Oxonians and Cambridgians — will hide themselves in the dens and the rocks of the mountains, and will say unto those mountains and rocks, *Fall on us and hide us from the face of the last thinker, for the great day of his wrath is come...*

And the *seventh* seal? When the seventh seal of thought is opened? No one knows what will happen then, W. says. No one can imagine it. Every enemy of thought shall seek death:

that's what has been prophesised. And they shall not find it. Every enemy of thought shall desire to die, and have death flee from them...

There will be disasters, W. says. Great mountains burning with fire will be cast into the sea, and the sea will become as churning blood.

The Leviathan will awaken, W. says. The Behemoth. And the Beast will reign in Babylon, the regenerated city. And the remnant who will survive, the 144,000 who will have the name of the last thinker written on their foreheads, will ready themselves for the last battle, for the war of Armageddon when Babylon is smashed and the Beast is vanquished.

And then a new city will appear in heaven, W. says. A new dispensation. The *University of New Jerusalem*: that's what they'll call it. The university where all are students, and all teachers. The university without courses or curricula, where each learns from the lips of the other. The *University of Speech*, where one heeds the other and is thereby awoken. The *University in Flight*, where what matters is to *move* with thought, to dance and sing with it, and not to remain still. The *University of the Periphery*, which will be at the edges of everywhere, and wherever you turn.

'*Meet me at the sea!*', W.'s text message reads, when I arrive at Plymouth airport. Over lunch at *Platters*, W. tells me the joyful news: his postgraduates are planning an occupation! They're going to take back the college campus!

There are only a few Plymouth postgraduates, W. says. Only a handful. But there were only a handful of Situationists! '*Give me a lever long enough, and a fulcrum on which to place it, and I shall move the world*', W. says, quoting Archimedes. Well, the Plymouth postgraduates are the lever, he says. And his college is the fulcrum. And the world really might be moved...

It's happening! It's really happening! W. can't contain his joy. Of course, we mustn't interfere, he says. It's *their* revolution, not ours. But they've asked us to speak, W. says. Well, they've asked *him* to speak. He's invited me along for some pathos, he says. Revolutions thrive on pathos, he says.

W. quotes Lenin: '*Revolution is a tough business. You can't make it wearing white gloves and with clean hands*'. — 'You can't make revolution in a blousy shirt, either', W. says. The linen look: is that what I'm going for? Of course, he's just as bad, W. says. He should have asked Sal to advise him on revolutionary chic.

Ice-creams, by the cannon pointing out at the Hoe. The Cita-
del, grey and looming at our backs. Light on the waves. Nice
weather for a revolution! Did the Communards on the barricades get *a good tan*? Were there blue skies above the revolutionaries when they stormed the Bastille?

You're supposed to carry an onion, to stop your eyes smart-
ing from tear gas, W. says. And you're supposed to wear an
extra vest, to stop plastic bullets. And you're supposed to wear
wrist bands and knee protectors like skateboarders, to keep
the police dogs off...

But we're going to turn up just as we are, W. decides. In
our finitude. Our vulnerability. They'll see our blousy shirts,
as they're raising their batons to strike us. They'll see our
podgy bodies and our spectacles. They'll see the *truth!*, W.
says. And then they'll swap sides, and join us on the barricades...

A taxi to the campus. The skeleton of the cathedral, hollowed out by Luftwaffe bombs in World War II... The broad boulevards of Abercrombie's city centre... The parkland surrounding the Plymouth Argyle football grounds... This is the last time we'll see Plymouth with our old eyes, W. says.

This time tomorrow, we'll probably be roaring through the city in the back of a police van, W. says. They'll show us on BBC Southwest, being bundled into cells.

And this time next week?, W. wonders. They'll have locked us up. We'll be prisoners of conscience. Political prisoners! Bono will dedicate a song to us. Our picture, like Ché's, will stare out from a thousand posters...

W's college, at the edge of Dartmoor.

Students smoking in small groups. The remnants of disposable barbeques. Spread blankets, and a portable MP3 player pounding out Jandek's *Modern Dances*. This is his kind of political protest, W. says.

W.'s disappointed that none of his sport science students have joined the occupation. He thought he might have been able to turn them. He thought they might have ended up on his side, armed with cricket bats and hockey sticks.

But his philosophy postgraduates are out in force, W. says. The last humanities students of the college! The brave remnant, the sign of righteousness on their foreheads, ready to confront the army of the Antichrist.

But there is no army. Only a lone security guard, sitting on a plastic chair.

Rain. We take refuge in the smokers' shelter. Where are the police?, W. wonders. Where are the university authorities? Even the security guard is putting his thermos flask away, and preparing to leave. W. waves at him, and he waves back. — 'Come and join the revolution!', W. shouts. But the security guard is too far away to hear.

Night. A fire in the empty carpark. Empty playing fields. The campus woods. Postgraduates, sitting on the kerb.

'*Since the destruction of the Temple, the divine inspiration has been withdrawn from the Prophets, and given to madmen and children*', W. says to our audience, quoting from the Talmud. 'And it's been given to idiots, too', he says. And then, under his breath: 'Go, fat boy!'

It will be like Chernobyl, our future, I tell the audience. And they will be like Chernobyl children, our descendants, each with his own deformity, each her own cancer.

That's how they'll know one another in future, I tell them: by their cancers. Everyone will have a different kind of cancer. One will have cancer of the spleen, the other cancer of the heart, a third cancer of the ears, and so on. And they'll die before they're teenagers, like Chernobyl children. They'll die with no one to care for them, gasping for air. They'll die alone and screaming, millions of them, billions of them, as the atmosphere boils away.

'Go on', W. says, *sotto voce*. 'Tell them about your vision'.

I see them building great cities at the Poles, I tell our audience. The last cities, after the destruction of the other ones, into which no one is allowed but the rich. They'll build *New Mumbai* in northern Siberia, when the old one drowns, I tell them. They'll build *New London* in northern Scandinavia, when the old one burns, I tell them. They'll build *New Mexico City* in the Western Antarctic, when the old one is razed in the coming wars, I tell them.

We'll die in our millions, I tell them. In our billions! Africa will have to be abandoned. India. China will become a dustbowl; America, a salt plain. We'll die slowly, in great agony, as the skies burn red. We'll sink down by the walls built to exclude us. We'll die by the laser swords of robot soldiers. We'll die of starvation and we'll die of exhaustion. We'll die of thirst, terrible thirst. We'll die of new diseases for which there are no names...

And *New Shanghai* will tower into Arctic skies, I tell our audience. *New Washington* will gleam like Canary Wharf in northern Alaska...

And our bodies will swell and rot in the blazing heat. Do you know what corpses smell like?, I ask our audience. They smell *sweet*, I tell them. There's a smell of rotting, yes, but there's a smell of sweetness, too.

'Pathos, more pathos!', W. whispers.

I see the money-makers still profiteering on the cindered husk of the earth, I tell our audience. I see *New Beetham Tower* in the New Manchester of the Arctic. I see *New Old Hulme* floating on the ice-free ocean...

I see celebrities on red carpets under hot, black skies, I tell our audience. I see helicopters circling in the burning sky. I see military putsches and crazed dictators. I see *Fascism 2.0*. I see *Fundamentalism Reloaded*. I see wars without end.

I see investors leaving earth in a swarm of rockets, I tell our audience. I see the mega-rich in orbit around a burning earth. I see them looking outward, out towards the stars, for new investment opportunities...

'Are they weeping yet?', W. asks. They're not weeping, I tell him. Okay, it's his turn, W. says.

'*In the dark times, will there still be singing?*', W. asks our audience, quoting Brecht. '*In the dark times, there will be singing about the dark times*'. As with song, so with speech, W.

says. 'The last covenant will be the covenant of speech', W. tells our audience, obscurely. 'Speech is our promise', he says, but no one really understands.

W. repeats to the audience something I've told him about my monk years. Every night, before dinner, the monks would bless the garden with incense. Incense would waft through the leaves. It would waft into the night and towards the animals of the night. Towards the city foxes and the barn owls. Towards the slugs and the snails and the rats. Incense would waft to the people of the night: to the prostitutes on the corner, and to the burglars who used the gardens as a run-through. To the junkies looking for their fix, and to the muggers waiting in their alleys.

This is what happens with speech, W. says. Whenever we speak, we speak to others. To the junkies and burglars. To the prostitutes on the corner. We speak to the outcasts, to the widows and the orphans. We speak to the city foxes! To the barn owls! We speak to the slugs and the snails and the rats! We address them, W. says. Our speech redeems them.

Here I am, that's what Moses said when God called his name, W. tells our audience. Here I am, that's what each of us says when we speak. Here I am, ready in response to the other, to all the others. Ready in response to God, to what remains of God.

God's people are prophets: Moses said that, W. tells our audience. Every person is a prophet: Amos said that. We are prophets in speech, W. says. We prophesise by speech. We save the world through our speech. We are messiahs, each of us, because of our capacity to speak.

And what does the messianic epoch mean but speech?,

W. says. What does it mean but the day of judgement that is announced in speech? Speech belongs to the Moment, W. says. Speech is touched with eternity...

W. reads out a quotation from his notebook:

> *I don't believe in materialism, this consumer society, this capitalism, this monstrosity that goes on here... I really do believe in something, and I call it 'a day will come'. And one day it will come. Well, it probably won't come, because they've already destroyed it for us, for so many thousands of years they've always destroyed it. It won't come and yet I believe in it. For if I can't believe in it, then I can't go on writing either.*

That's Ingeborg Bachmann, W. tells our audience. A day will come — the day *is* coming, every time we speak. Tomorrow, W. says, the police will come and break up our occupation. But there is another tomorrow; another *kind* of tomorrow. Tomorrow it was May, W. says. And tomorrow it will be May again...

Midnight. — 'The messianic era is about to begin', W. says quietly, almost to himself. Then he shouts it out, for all the occupation to hear: 'The apocalypse is upon us!' And then, 'Let's drink to it!', he cries, but the college bar's stopped serving.

12.06 AM. W. catches a taxi back to his house on the other side of the city, to fetch the entire contents of his drinks cabinet. — 'Drink for his friends!', he says, unloading a boot full of booze. 'Drink for everyone!' It might be his finest hour, W. says.

1.51 AM. Sitting out in the quad, we drink W.'s bottles of Plymouth Gin and Plymouth Sloe Gin. We even drink his rare bottle of Plymouth *Damson* Gin, which they haven't made for a number of years, because they can't find good quality fruit. And we drink one of his treasures: Plymouth Navy Strength Gin in the *old* bottle, before the redesign: gin at 90 proof, made that strong so as not to be inadvertently ignited by cannon gunpowder. That was the one time he was refused a drink at the Plymouth Gin cocktail bar, W. says: when, already drunk, he asked for a Martini made from Navy Strength Gin.

Then, we drink a bottle of Zwack Unicum, a Hungarian liqueur that tastes like toothpaste, from a bottle shaped like a hand grenade. It's really the property of the *Plymouth Béla Tarr Society*, W. says, one of whose members brought it back from the *puszta*, the great central plain of Hungary. We drink a round of Slivovitz, the famous plum brandy from Eastern Europe — *drink* Eastern European, *think* Eastern European, W. says — and then a round of Becherovka, a kind of nutmeg liquor from the Czech Republic. And then we drink several bottles of warm Chablis — a terrible waste, W. says, since it should be served ice-cold with turbot. But how else is he going to keep us all drunk?

2.13 AM. Alcohol makes people *speak*, that's its greatness, W. says. It makes them religious, political, even as it shows them the *impossibility* of religion and the *impossibility* of politics. Drinking carries you through despair, W. says. Through it, and out beyond it, if you are prepared to keep drinking right all through the night.

2.52 AM. We have to libate the palm trees!, W. tells us. I didn't know there were palm trees on campus, but W. assures me they exist. And there they are — palm trees in a grove, over which we pour a half-bottle of Mara Schino, a liqueur from old Yugoslavia that is too disgusting even for us to drink.

3.01 AM. The hour of the wolf. We hunt for the legendary Plymouth Pear in the campus woods. We talk of Beckett and Arhika, drunk in Paris. We talk of Gombrowicz in Argentina, Flusser in Brazil ... were they drinkers?, W. wonders. They were exiles, of course, but drinkers?

W. opens his notebook. *'The exile is a man of a coming future world...'*: that's Flusser, he says.

'Nothing in my background could have prepared me for the huge role alcohol played in these people's lives': that's Arhika's wife in her memoir, W. says. And Gombrowicz, what did Gombrowicz write? W. has nothing of relevance in his notebook.

W. tells the postgraduates an anecdote from the life of Debord. There was a poster near Chez Moineau, which read *Alcohol kills slowly*, W. says. *'We don't give a fuck. We've got the time'*, Debord scrawled over it...

We've got the time. Life is long, not short, W. says. Life is terribly long... It's too long!... *To live without a lifetime*, I read from my notebook. *To die forsaken by death...*

3.15 AM. A grove in the wood. This is where we should be buried, W. says. This is where they should set our graves. *Here lies W. — a friend of thought. Here lies Lars — a friend of a friend of thought.*

3.20 AM. We've never lived: W. is haunted by that thought. We've never lived! We were never alive, not for one moment! That's W.'s horror.

Life! We can barely sit at a table, W. says. What do we know about life?

3.29 AM. We need to discover a new *discipline* of drinking, to drink until our teeth are stained red from wine, W. says. *In vino veritas*, he says. In *vino*, all we'll ever know of *veritas*, he says.

I read from my notebook. *A man who drinks is interplanetary*, Duras said. *He moves through interstellar space.* We're astronauts, we agree. Cosmonauts! *Alcohol doesn't console, it doesn't fill up anyone's psychological gaps, all it replaces is the lack of God*, Duras said. The lack of God! We know what she means. Our lives! Our voids! Oh God, what we might have been! Oh God, what in fact we are!

3.35 AM. We piss on the pebble-dashed wall of the V.C.'s house. — *'Babylon is falling'*, W. says, quoting Winstanley. *Babylon the great is falling*, I say, quoting Prince Far-I.

3.57 AM. He can hear voices, W. says. *Go towards the light*, that's what they're telling him. Meanwhile, he has the sensation of floating above his body. Has he died? Has the world ended? Is this the apocalypse, or not?

4.20 AM. Turn towards the light, that's the advice to the departing soul in the Tibetan Book of the Dead, W. says. But he sees no light, he says, only darkness.

4.28 AM. W. thinks of Lenin, after his stroke, being wheeled along in his basket chair, his brain dying, a twisted half-smile on his face, no longer able to say the words *peasant* and *worker*, no longer understanding the words *people* and *revolution*.

He thinks of Lenin, with only a few months to live, regressed to his second infancy, his brain turning into cottage-cheese-like mush, suffering paralytic attacks and spasms, whispering the nonsense phrase, *vot-vot*, to express agreement or disagreement, to make a request or to vent frustration. *Vot-vot, vot-vot…*

4.40 AM. Dawn. Birds singing.

We need to wait, W. tells the postgraduates, as we watch the first plane take off from Plymouth Airport. We need to be watchful, and as watchmen, drunk. Above all, we need to drink!, W. tells the postgraduates, filling their cups. We need to perfect a continual drunkenness, he tells them. A vigilant drunkenness! A *sober* drunkenness!

There's no point in going to sleep, W. tells the Plymouth postgraduates. What use is sleep to us? We must stay awake, ever-watchful. We must stand watch for signs of revolution. We must be like the pillar saints, waiting for God. We must imitate Saint Anthony in the desert, wrestling with his demons. And above all we must wait, and wait together. Above all!

God gives the sky the dimensions of His absence, I quote from Jabès. God… he doesn't know what God means, W. says.

4.44 AM. He wishes he could summon the former Essex post-graduates to his side, W. says. He wishes he could blow a great horn, like that guy in *Anchorman*, and have them all come running.

The scattered tribes would be reunited! The exiles would be ingathered from foreign lands, ready for the last battle...

4.52 AM. W. thinks of Marx on his deathbed, cursing the country he had adopted. '*England is the rock against which revolutionary waves break, the country where the new society is stifled even in the womb*'. Drat England!, Marx said. Drat Britain!

W. thinks of Debord, shooting himself in the heart at his house in the Auvergne. He thinks of Weil, starving herself to death. He thinks of Duras, drying out in one clinic, then another ... Drat the world!, W. says. Drat our times!

5.00 AM. If only we could sleep, really sleep, W. says. If only we could *rest*.

W. dreams of the profound slumber from which we would rise reborn, ready for the morning, ready for work. He dreams of the great day that would follow our night of rest, and of the great ideas that would flash above us like diurnal stars.

How is it still alive in him, the belief that he might *wake into genius?*, W. says. How is it that he still believes, despite everything, that he is a *man of thought*?

5.40 AM. We think with our tears, with our sadnesses, W. says. We think from our humiliations, our desperations...

5.43 AM. Thought is the hangman, our hangman, W. says. Thought has its nooses ready, just for us.

5.55 AM. Really, thought is a kind of *assault*, W. says.

6.02 AM. *To think is to stray. To think is to err greatly*: who was it said that?, W. wonders. Well, there's erring and *erring*. There's straying and *straying*, W. says.

6.11 AM. In the end, thought is dread, W. says. It is indistinguishable from dread.

6.44 AM. 'Are they coming for us?', W. asks. — 'Can you hear sirens?' No one's coming, I tell him. I can hear nothing but birdsong and faraway cars.

7.00 AM. All around us, on the grass, the Plymouth postgraduates are sleeping. All of God's children are asleep.

What are they dreaming of?, we wonder. Of wide, high Dartmoor, W. hopes. Of cider made from the apples of the moor. Of songs of peace and gentleness sung on the moor. And of Plymouth Sound, seen all the way from the moor, glinting like utopia.

LARS IYER is a lecturer in philosophy at the Newcastle University. He is the author of *Spurious*, which was *3:AM Magazine*'s Book of the Year in 2011, *Dogma*, two books on Blanchot *(Blanchot's Communism: Art, Philosophy, and the Political* and *Blanchot's Vigilance: Literature, Phenomenology, and the Ethical*), and his blog Spurious. He is also a contributor to Britain's leading literary blog, *Ready, Steady, Book*. His literary manifesto, "Nude in Your Hot Tub, Facing the Abyss" appeared in *Post Road* and *The White Review*.

READ THE FIRST TWO BOOKS
IN THE ACCLAIMED SERIES

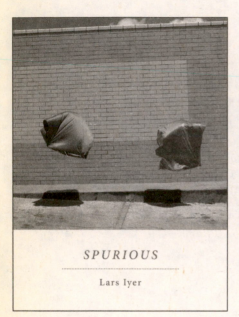

SPURIOUS

Lars Iyer

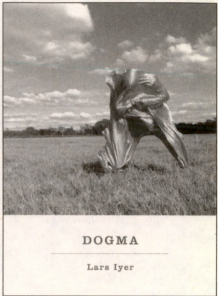

DOGMA

Lars Iyer